Paddy Joe
and Tomkin's Folly

Paddy Joe
and Tomkin's Folly

Joyce Stranger

PELHAM BOOKS

First published in Great Britain by Pelham Books Ltd
52 Bedford Square, London WC1B 3EF

Copyright © 1979 Joyce Stranger Limited

ISBN 0 7207 1129 0

Typeset in Great Britain by
the Northumberland Press Ltd, Gateshead, Tyne and Wear
Printed and Bound in Great Britain by
Billing & Sons Limited,
Guildford, London and Worcester

Dedicated to my grandson Jonathan, and my granddaughter Mairi and also to Thomas, who is alive and well and living in Prestbury with the Woodwards who told me this story.

Acknowledgement

The quotation on page 65 from "In the Pride of his Youth" from *Plain Tales from the Hills* by Rudyard Kipling, is reproduced by courtesy of the National Trust.

Chapter One

"What's the matter with you all?" Tomkin shouted, almost beside himself with rage.

Paddy Joe looked at him in astonishment. The little lop-lipped, brown-faced man rarely lost his temper, and certainly not when the Colonel was present. But somehow this conference was not going well.

"I should have thought it was obvious," Lisa Mabley said wearily. She pushed her dark hair away from her eyes, and stared at them sombrely. "We can't meet our bills at all. Hay for the horses, feed for the dogs; we need new fencing. We have to cut back; have to sell some of our older dogs. Have to get rid of the horses. All of them," she added, looking pointedly at Paddy Joe.

Paddy Joe stared back at her, dark eyes angry. He had only owned his horse Shadowfax for ten months, but in that time they had formed a complete partnership, and Paddy Joe had plans. He had built himself five jumps in the biggest field and there he and the horse practised nightly.

"Look," Tomkin said, controlling himself with an immense effort. "It's no use being defeatist. Cut back; and then what? No foals to sell; no pups to sell; no dogs to campaign to become champions. Paddy Joe's beginning to make himself known with Storm and Gale; he won his class last week with Storm, and came fifth with Gale. He'll go places."

"I said we had to cut back on showing," the Colonel said. "It's costing far too much. Entry fees and petrol alone add up to about three pounds a week. It's ridiculous. And that's just for Paddy Joe. The Breed shows add up to so much it frightens me."

The conversation was frightening Paddy Joe. He looked at the solemn faces; at the Colonel, white haired and white moustached, looking older than his age since the slight stroke he had had five months before. The old man had fought back grimly, and was now riding again, although at first Paddy Joe had not believed the Colonel would even walk again. He was stooping a little now, but his vivid blue eyes were still alight with life, and he could work as long a day as the rest of them.

Lisa Mabley was dressed today in vivid blue; she had been economising on hair appointments and there were grey streaks showing that had not been apparent before. She was looking down at the pad before her, drawing dogs' heads; large Alsatian heads, with prick ears and dark eyes. She could not decide which dogs to sell. They were all part of her life.

2

Without them, she would have little left. She thought briefly of her husband, who had died a few years before, from an old war injury that had never healed completely. She pushed the thought away and stabbed at the paper, breaking the pencil lead.

Debbie, soon to leave school, was hiding behind her hair, which flowed, long and dark, over her shoulders. Her throat ached at the thought of selling even one of the dogs. It was worse than death. You knew where they had gone then, but you never knew when one was sold whether it was going to a good owner or a bad one; whether it would mind leaving the home it had known for so long; or would fret and never settle. Two dogs had been sold recently and both had been returned as unsuitable.

On enquiry Debbie found both had been treated with total lack of either sympathy or understanding.

Chris, the youngest of all of them, sat watching. He wanted, passionately, to shout and scream that nothing was fair. It wasn't their fault that prices were rising all the time. The month's vet bill hadn't been paid. One of the horses had injured a leg; one of the dogs had cut a pad on glass when racing through the shallow water of the river. Always other people, making trouble all the time.

Paddy Joe was tall and dark and growing fast. Chris, small and fair, felt inadequate beside him, left behind in the race to adulthood. But maybe being an adult wasn't fun either. His mother looked as if she would cry, any minute. The Colonel looked angry and Tomkin was angry, almost too angry to speak clearly.

"If you can think of any other way ..." the Colonel said. He couldn't bear the thought of selling any of the animals; or of making changes. But changes had to be made. His own income was falling all the time in comparison with the rest of the world's. And nobody would give an old man work. There was no question of that.

"It's a question of cunning," Tomkin said. "We use our wits. No use relying on anyone else to pull our irons out of the fire." Tomkin was seldom original. "They're not going to. It's up to us. It always was, only people today believe in a cockeyed God that's going to give them more money if they ask for it, or fight for it, or strike for it. Ask and ye shall receive. Well, it's not like that for us. We've no one to stretch our hands out to. The Government doesn't care about folk like us. They won't let us starve, or get sick, but they won't let us make a go of what we're doing either. So we outwit the lot of them."

"It's easy to talk," Debbie said.

"It's talking that's got the world where it is," Tomkin said savagely. "We're going to *do*. And I'll tell you what we're going to do. There's that land and house of old Cockshoot's up for auction next week. It's alongside Deep Hollow. Nineteen acres and a house. We can sell Brandings and move in there."

"The house is in terrible condition," the Colonel said.

"So we get it for a song," Tomkin said. "And we do it up ourselves. We can move into the flat over the stables at Deep Hollow while we work. Lisa won't mind."

4

Lisa shook her head, too bemused to speak.

"We'll have the money from the sale of the house; it should fetch quite a bit. And we grow our own hay; and turn over some of the fields to crops which we can sell. There's a good little tractor going cheap at the garage. Ned offered it me a few days ago. Needs some repairs but I can do those. And Chris is good at finding things out from his school pals; he can scout for us. We'll need decent second-hand stuff; stones and bricks and paving stones; fencing and wood; and we do every scrap ourselves. Debbie could leave school and go to secretarial college and get a job as soon as she can; that would help with the bills."

"I can do more than that," Debbie said. "I can baby sit, and wash up at the hotel in the village; and I could work in the supermarket or one of the shops in the town on a Saturday."

"I might find something to do," Chris said. "Maybe wash cars, or help at the garage."

"And I can help in the pub at night," Tomkin added. "They need another barman. I'm a dab hand at mixing drinks."

Paddy Joe frowned. He seemed to have little to offer, and then he remembered that it would soon be haymaking time.

"I can help hay make," he said.

"There's fruit picking too," Tomkin said. "And potato lifting. And you could maybe get a holiday job on one of the local farms. They're always short of labour. It'd help too, if you want to be a vet. Need to know about cattle and sheep and pigs, as well as dogs and cats and horses."

5

"You need to know about chickens and turkeys and ducks and geese and rabbits and mice and hamsters and hawks and guinea pigs and gerbils and goldfish," Chris said. "You could get jobs with all of those."

"I'll work on a goldfish farm," Paddy Joe said.

The atmosphere had lightened at the prospect of ways of getting out of their difficulties instead of going under. Lisa was scribbling figures on her pad, and so was the Colonel, both busy calculating how much it cost to run Deep Hollow, for rates and electricity and gas; for food for dogs and horses; for vet bills and emergencies; for repairs and clothes for all of them. It came to a formidable amount, even allowing for the fact that everyone now dressed in jeans and shirts when not in school uniform.

"I don't believe it," Lisa said, looking at her calculations. "It would keep the Queen for a year, let alone us."

"Hay at £30 a ton," the Colonel said; he frowned. "The last telephone bill was over £100; we're going to have to cut down on that."

"We'd better train the dogs to act as messengers," Chris said.

"Or buy some pigeons and use those," Paddy Joe said. "If I work on a farm I might get £10 a week in the holidays; and Chris could get about £5; and Debbie would maybe get £12 or so and tips; and Tomkin would bring in what? About £15 a week? That's £42 extra."

"Less tax," the Colonel said. "Paddy Joe's income will be added to mine. Tomkin might not have to pay tax. I don't seem to have been paying him much

6

more than pocket money for months; I always meant...."

"Don't want more," Tomkin said. "I leave you and get a job and it pays well and I live in digs, belonging nowhere. I said I was part of the family, didn't I? Of course, if you don't want me," he added, suddenly forlorn.

"Don't be an ass, man," the Colonel said irritably and Tomkin grinned as if he had been given the highest compliment possible.

"That's it, then," he said, settling his steel-rimmed glasses more firmly as they kept slipping down his nose. "We get our thinking caps on. Any way of making money legitimately goes."

"You used to make super soft toys when we were little, Mum," Debbie said. "We could make those and sell them to the local shops."

"We'd need to get hold of cheap materials or there's no profit in that," Lisa said.

"OK. Shoot me down in flames. I was only trying," Debbie said.

"Oh Debbie," Lisa said helplessly. She and Debbie always seemed to be at odds these days. She hadn't meant to sound off-putting.

"Let's go and look at the land next door, and that house," the Colonel said. "It might be practicable to renovate it. Maybe we could buy the land and sell the house to someone else."

"And where do we get the money to buy the land if we don't sell our present house?" Tomkin said.

Paddy Joe led the way into the yard outside. He

looked at Deep Hollow as if he were seeing it for the first time. The redbrick farmhouse sprawled in the corner of the cobbled yard. There were dog pens everywhere, but all were in need of repair. They couldn't be patched up much longer and still be secure. The big run needed concreting. The spring had been unusually wet and the grass had vanished. The dogs were running on mud, and had not improved the appearance of the place by digging holes in a number of unlikely corners.

Shadowfax, Paddy Joe's horse, watched them from over the half door of the stable. His wise head seemed to be questioning Paddy Joe. Are we practising tonight? But there were more important considerations.

The three big fields next door were easily reached through a shared gate. Paddy Joe pushed it open and the hinges groaned. The owner of the land had died the year before and now it was for sale. The grass was knee high and there were giant purple thistles everywhere.

They walked through the long grass, and Paddy Joe, turning his head, saw a wave in the grass behind him, and grinned. His two dogs were there: Storm now growing very wise as he was almost seven, and little Gale, dainty and pretty, soon to be mated and produce her first litter. If all went well. Behind them was a smaller ripple that was, Paddy Joe knew, caused by Mad Cat, the "tom" cat that had proved to be a female, and had had kittens. Behind her, in the grass, too small to make even a ripple, would be Awful, the kitten that they had kept, and that had his mother's habit of following the dogs everywhere. He had grown into a very tiny cat. Paddy Joe rarely went out without a procession. If he didn't want the cats, they had to be shut in.

The second field was divided into three parts. A lane led into the top third, which was shielded by an overgrown hawthorn hedge. Paddy Joe had never been further than this, but as he went through the archway that had once covered a gate, he found himself in an abandoned garden, where roses rioted in a tangle of grass, and lupins flaunted themselves among ragwort and nettles and thistles.

The house was even more dilapidated than he had expected. When they went inside, the dust rose in eddies round their feet. The staircase was still intact, and the upstairs proved to be a maze of tiny rooms, one leading off the other, some so small that they seemed no larger than cupboards.

Tomkin was tapping walls and looking at the woodwork.

"We'd have to gut the whole inside," he said. "Half these partitions are flimsy; not part of the original structure of the house. We can have three big rooms up here and a bathroom."

He led the way downstairs again. Lisa was looking at a Victorian fireplace.

"There's an older fireplace behind this," she said. "Someone's been digging to see. I think you'd find an ingle nook and one of those lovely wide hearths. This room was once all one room. You could make a big room with a low ceiling, rather like my living room. It has got possibilities."

The Colonel was leaning on his stick, his mouth tight.

"It's crazy," he said. "It would take us years to make it habitable."

"Look," Tomkin said. "Years ago when I was a scoutmaster we got the lads building a scout hut. Every bit of it, from the foundations up and they made a splendid job. We can involve the local troops; they'd jump at it. Imagine helping to build a house. I bet you we can get all the help we want and have fun doing it. The auction's next week; and if it's ready money you want, there's my savings to put down for a deposit. And we can talk to the bank manager; and get a bridging loan till we sell our house. You won't mind the house being sold, Paddy Joe?"

Paddy Joe shook his head. It had been his grandmother's house, where he had lived since he was a year old when his parents had been killed in a plane crash. His grandmother had been killed by a car, and the Colonel had adopted him and Storm; he had sold his own cottage, which was too small for all of them, and moved in with Paddy Joe, buying the house from him and putting the money in the bank to pay for the boy's keep and education. The bank had managed the funds, which were made into a trust but the income from that was dwindling and it looked very much as if Paddy Joe might never be a vet. Six years' training was a very long time. And during that time he couldn't earn money to help out – they might not manage alone.

They had to do something. And this seemed as if

it might be worth doing. He looked at the house again. Damp walls and dirty rooms with paper falling from the ceilings. An age old smell of decay and mould.

There was a sudden crash and a loud yell.

Everyone ran outside, into the barn where Chris was picking himself up from a heap of hay.

"Good job that was there," he said ruefully. "I fell through the ceiling. It's all rotten. But the other two are jolly good barns and would make wonderful byres and stables. You could keep cows. And look at the stuff stored in them. They're dry as a bone. Drier than the house."

"You wouldn't like us to have tigers and elephants, too?" the Colonel asked acidly, still overwhelmed by the magnitude of the task they were apparently all hellbent on taking on.

"You could have a safari park then," Chris said. "It would be fun naming elephants."

"We've enough on our plate," Lisa said. "We have to be practical. I think maybe Tomkin has a point; you should get about three times as much for the house you live in now as you need to pay for this."

'We'll go to the auction," the Colonel said. "And we'll put our own top price on it. I'm not paying through the nose for a pig in a poke."

"Nothing venture, nothing win," Tomkin said, preferring as always to have the last word. He had a store of sayings for every occasion. Sometimes he used a new one, and Paddy Joe, standing staring at nothing, wondering if they were all crazy, was the target for one of these.

"Don't stand there like a pot cat," Tomkin said irritably. "Shift yourself, Paddy Joe. There's work to do and that horse of yours hasn't been cleaned out or fed yet, and there's all the dogs to feed."

Tomkin was always pushing, Paddy Joe thought irritably, as he fetched the shovel and the broom and the wheelbarrow, and went into the stable to attend to Shadowfax, who greeted him by dropping his long wet tongue into the palm of Paddy Joe's hand, sure that this welcome was as much of a pleasure to his master as it was to him.

"Move over, you old nut," Paddy Joe said, slapping the horse on the side of his face with a gentle hand. The horse pushed back and nuzzled him. Paddy Joe was suddenly and inexplicably elated and began to whistle as he worked.

Chapter Two

Life changed all the time. Paddy Joe, riding his horse down the lanes, after school, reined in and looked across the fields. He was restless, wanting something to happen, anything, wanting the years to pass, and school to end, wanting to be a vet at last and part of the world, instead of being on the edge of adult life.

He wished Tomkin would stop nagging him. He wished the Colonel was not so irritable. He wished that they had as much money as in the years when he was young, and nothing seemed a problem. He wished Debbie would take more notice of him; she enraged him beyond measure by treating him as if he were the same age as Chris, instead of being almost the same age as she was.

He turned the horse, and set his head at the hedge beyond the road, thundering over the tarmac, soaring into the air, releasing anger in a mad leap that he knew he should never have attempted.

He knew it with even greater certainty as he saw the ground below him. Someone had been digging a ditch where no ditch had been the day before. The horse was going to land badly, hind hooves down and fore hooves up and there was nothing whatever he could do about it.

The horse landed, and slipped, rolling over. Paddy Joe jumped clear, furious at himself. He could not, for that moment, look at Shadowfax, who was on his side, panting, his great eyes rolling. Suppose he'd broken a leg; suppose he had to be shot; Paddy Joe, always dreaming up disasters, knew he could not face Tomkin and the Colonel. He would have to tell Lisa and ask her to break the news for him. Lisa was always sympathetic; Paddy Joe often envied Chris and Debbie for having a mother when he had none. He had two fathers though as Chris never tired of pointing out.

The horse levered himself upright. Paddy Joe stood beside him, watching, praying under his breath. "I'll never jump like that again if only he's all right."

But when the animal began to walk, there was an ominous limp. Paddy Joe knelt and felt the leg. He was sure nothing was broken. A pulled tendon perhaps. Which meant the vet and meant treatment and extra care; and meant the rough side of Tomkin's tongue. Perhaps he could pretend they had fallen down a rabbit hole. But someone might have seen them. And it was no use trying to cover up.

Nothing ever went right.

Paddy Joe walked home beside his limping horse,

cursing his own stupidity. When he told Tomkin, Tomkin would say: "Look before you leap. How many times have I told you? Think on, Paddy Joe."

Paddy Joe would run away to sea; or join the army. Everyone thought he was eighteen, although he was not yet seventeen. He was taller than any of them now, level with the Colonel, looking down on Tomkin, surprised to find the little man so small. Lisa and Debbie had shrunk too, but Chris was catching him up fast and would be broader and heavier as well. Paddy Joe was the lean type.

"Let me have about me men who are fat. Yon Cassius has a lean and hungry look," Chris said, pedalling silently behind him so that Paddy Joe jumped and Shadowfax reared.

"Idiot," Paddy Joe said, far more angrily than he had intended, letting out some of the fury he felt with himself, on Chris. "You should know better than to do that behind a horse. Anyway you've got it wrong."

"I haven't," Chris said. He dismounted, and wheeled his bike alongside Paddy Joe. "What's he done?"

Paddy Joe said nothing for a moment. He watched a bird soar over the trees.

The beating wings moved rapidly, and then the flight tailed into a long slow glide. A peregrine, or he was a Dutchman, but better keep that dark or Chris would blab it all round the school. It might be nesting.

"What did you do?" Chris repeated, irritated by

Paddy Joe's silence. Once they had chattered together endlessly, but now Paddy Joe often looked through him, as if he were tired of childishness and thinking of much more important things. Everyone seemed to ignore Chris, who seldom thought deeply or appreciated other people's viewpoints, seeing what he wanted, and going for it, wholeheartedly, ignoring obstacles.

Paddy Joe had been like that once. Now he felt older and wiser, and found Chris childish.

"I jumped the hedge. Some fool had been ditching, and Shadowfax fell," Paddy Joe said at last.

"Tomkin'll have your hide," Chris said. "He's limping badly. Sure it's not broken?"

"He couldn't walk if it was broken," Paddy Joe said, wishing he could jump on the horse and ride away from Chris's chatter. "Look, your mother will be worrying. Why don't you ride on? I can't go fast."

"OK, if you feel like that," Chris said. "I don't know what's up with the lot of you; Tomkin's as ratty as old Nick; the Colonel roars if you open your mouth. Mother sits looking as if the end of the world was tomorrow and Debbie's so besotted about that farm student you can't get any sense out of her."

"He's an idiot," Paddy Joe said, and Chris grinned to himself and rode off, having succeeded in being just as provoking as he'd intended. Paddy Joe was jealous of anyone Debbie dated, and Chris betted Paddy Joe didn't even know why.

Paddy Joe looked at the departing back and

suddenly found himself wishing Chris would fall off, not to hurt himself, but just to take some of the cockiness out of him.

He stopped to rest the horse, and Shadowfax dipped his head to graze. Paddy Joe glanced round him, at green fields edged with summer trees, at the slope of a hill, and high above it, the soaring bird. He envied it its freedom, with the long sky to glide in, and no responsibility of any sort. He wished he were a prince, long ago, with a bird on his fist, releasing the bird to fly free, watching it hunt for him and then return, swinging out of the sky, more splendid than earthbound creatures, with its proud head and bright eye, and confiding expression, subject only to him, obeying no other man.

It was time to go on. If only he hadn't had that extra hour free this afternoon, hadn't been tempted to ride in the sun, hadn't been tempted by that high hedge, and his own feeling of wildness, longing for an endless gallop that went on and on, releasing him from the need to conform to a world that frowned on all expressions of high spirits.

Tomkin was walking across the cobbled yard, carrying a bale of hay. He turned and watched the horse limping, moving painfully across the ground. His thin lips tightened, and his eyes were angry as he looked at Paddy Joe.

"You went out of here like a bat out of hell," he said. "I knew there'd be trouble. How many times have I told you? What did you do?"

"Jumped the hedge; there was a new ditch since yesterday. I've jumped it a dozen times before,"

Paddy Joe said. He felt like a small boy again, and hated the feeling.

"There could have been people picnicking; or a dog; or cattle; things don't stay the same for ever, even for twelve hours," Tomkin said, fighting a desire to clip Paddy Joe good and hard across the ears. "Get in and get your homework done. I'll see to the horse. I don't trust you to do it properly. You skimped his bedding last night; I've told you before."

"I was trying to economise; you're all on about it all the time," Paddy Joe said, resenting the unfairness.

"We don't skimp on the animals. On ourselves yes, on them, no. And don't annoy the Colonel. He's got gout, again."

Which meant even more roaring, Paddy Joe thought. He went up to his room and flung himself down on the bed, staring at nothing. He hadn't made his bed before he went out. The room needed tidying and dusting, and Tomkin would grumble if that weren't done either. He expected the place to be kept with the spartan neatness of a barracks, long years in the army making him forget that they were not subject to discipline now.

Paddy Joe straightened the bedding, neatened the cover, and put away his clothes. Sunshine flickered on the leaves outside his window, and a sudden angry chatter of little birds told him the short eared owl was about again. He always hunted in broad daylight. Somewhere beyond the tree his round winged body was hovering, hunting for prey in the grass. He was a regular visitor, combing the meadow at breakfast time and tea time, or brooding on a post, his head swivelling as he watched the telltale ripple in the long grass.

Paddy Joe dropped into the battered leather armchair that the Colonel had given him, so that he could use his bedroom as a private sitting room of his own, and stared at the sky. He heard the sounds from outside; Tomkin soothing the horse, the stamp of a hoof on the ground, the Colonel, walking heavily, his stick tapping, his voice gruff as he asked a question. Tomkin's voice was lighter and sharper.

Paddy Joe sighed. It might be as well if he got supper; Tomkin would be busy with Shadowfax. And he had forgotten about the dogs. They should have come to greet him, but neither had appeared. It wasn't like Storm to ignore him; nor Gale. So they had been shut in; and that meant that they had been mischievous.

Paddy Joe moved fast, knowing it would be better if he provided a really good meal, showing willing; if he *and* the dogs were in trouble....

He ran downstairs. Mad Cat was sitting in the sunshine on the sill, washing himself with careful concentration. Herself. It was hard to remember Mad Cat was a she. Tomkin had had her spayed, after the kittens were born. Awful, her firstborn, was stretched on the cobbles, rolling in the sun.

There was a whimper from outside.

The dogs were shut in the outhouse. But why? Better not let them free. He was in enough bother. The vet might have to come and give Shadowfax an injection; and the horse would need resting; and goodness knows how bad the injury was.

Paddy Joe rummaged in the deep freeze. If he cooked steak; that would earn him the accusation of extravagance; so it had better be mince. He chopped an onion, and put it on to fry, watching with careful concentration. He hunted for flavourings, mixing in a number of unlikely ingredients with a steady hand. Chris, who wanted to be a chef, had given him the recipe, but he had never had a chance to try it before.

Tomkin came into the kitchen just as Paddy Joe was putting the food in the oven.

"Just as well you started that," Tomkin said. "I haven't had a minute all day. That horse is shoulder lame; when he's cooled off he needs the hose running on him for an hour; and you've other work to do besides. You left the field gate open this morning when you went to school."

Paddy Joe thought back. He had been late for the bus, he'd had to run across the five acre, where Tomkin exercised the dogs, and yes, he had forgotten to shut the gate as he sprinted to make the corner, afraid the driver would pass him.

"Did the dogs get out?" Paddy Joe asked.

"No. Moffat's pigs got in. All six of them. Through the kitchen garden, into the rose garden and left enough muck on the lawn to manure the place for a year."

"Free manure," Paddy Joe said hopefully, wondering why Tomkin looked so grim.

"That's what the dogs thought," Tomkin said. "They rolled. Both of them. They stink to high heaven so when you've made the pudding and laid the cloth you can go and bath them, and neither one comes in here till it smells like my mother's lavender press. I've put them in the empty outhouse on straw; Storm's the worst; it's down to his skin. Gale was daintier. It's only on her back; he's plastered. And put on old clothes; they'll need soaking afterwards."

Paddy Joe chopped fruit for a fruit salad, took cream out of the freezer and put it on top of the stove to defrost, and laid the table. He sighed as he fetched the big tin bath and filled it with tepid water and with dog shampoo. Both dogs loved the river but they loathed being bathed. He'd better do Gale first.

He sighed again as he walked towards the outhouse. She wasn't at all an easy bitch; she was always anxious, desperately afraid she might have done wrong, and after being shut in all afternoon she'd know she had done wrong, and be tricky to handle. She became awkward and unable to understand what he wanted of her when she was uncertain of herself, unlike Storm who was bold and full of confidence and never did believe anyone could possibly not want him, whether he was as clean as any dog could be, or covered in muck.

Paddy Joe opened the door, shouting: STORM, STAY, but Storm and Gale erupted together, stinking so much that Paddy Joe caught his breath. Storm led the way, leaping over the gate, back into the garden that had been so gloriously scented only that morning. He lay on his back, his face blissful, rubbing himself on the grass that Tomkin had cleared.

Paddy Joe, angry with the dog, fetched the bench-
ing collar and a rope and tied him to a tree, before
calling to Gale.

Some of his irritation must have appeared in his
voice, as instead of coming she ran into the bushes and
hid herself, refusing to emerge from the thorny
thicket in which she had found sanctuary.

It was half an hour before Paddy Joe managed
to entice her to him with a hunk of cheese. Storm,
wanting some too, sat and whined.

"Shut that damned dog up," the Colonel shouted,
from somewhere inside the house.

Storm barked, not recognising the Colonel's voice,
sure an intruder had got in.

"Hateful dog, be quiet," Paddy Joe yelled and
Storm, astounded, dropped to the ground, his nose
on his paws, aware that he had better not transgress
again as even Paddy Joe was in a bad mood and it
was always better for a dog to obey when that
happened.

Gale, frightened afresh by the shouting, slipped out
of the water, sending a shower over Paddy Joe, and
raced into the outhouse where she crouched on the
straw, dirtying herself all over again as she lay
where Storm had been lying. He had left muck
behind him. It clung to her wet fur.

Paddy Joe put on her lead and dragged her
back, the bitch resisting at every step.

"Come on, girl. Good girl, come on then," Paddy
Joe said, using the softest voice he could put on, knowing how she hated noise. She ran from fights; she
cowered when people argued noisily; she clung to

Storm, never wanting to be alone. The big dog guarded her, and kept intruders away, not from the property, Tomkin said, but from Gale.

By the time she was clean Paddy Joe was drenched. He towelled her as dry as he could and put her in a clean stall in the stable to finish drying off.

Now it was time for Storm.

Storm had grown massive in the past two years. He was a boldly coloured dog, his head broad-browed, his muzzle beautifully marked, his eyes large, his big ears set well on his head. No one knew his pedigree as he had been rescued, but he had developed into a fine dog, and many of those who knew the German Shepherd dog well thought they could trace his ancestry. Each breeder put his own mark on the dogs he bred; and there were charac-teristics that came through, even after generations of breeding.

He danced out of the shadows, leaping at Paddy Joe, delighted to see him. Paddy Joe gasped at the reek. It was going to be an all time battle to get Storm clean. As Paddy Joe pulled, the dog pulled back, eyeing the water with dislike.

"The Colonel's looking after the supper," Tomkin said, appearing rather like a genie round the corner of the house, holding the hose. "Hold him still and I'll hose him; then you can soap him, and we'll hose him again. Use the scrubbing brush; you'll never get him into the water in that mood. He's gone fey. Funny how they love to smear themselves in muck. Damned pigs." The Moffat pigs had been a sore point for years. They were apt to break out and wander as the fields were not fenced properly round the small-holding, and the hedges grew sparsely, and were never improved or cut. Moffat himself was a local character, who spent half his life drunk and the other half repenting, while his wife, a thin angry-tongued woman, kept the place together by working so hard that she looked twenty years older than her actual age.

"The auction's on Thursday," Tomkin added, directing the hose at the dog, who danced to dodge it, but was held too firmly. Paddy Joe was caught in the spray and shivered with the shock of the water. The sun was lower and the shadows lengthening; they were late with supper tonight. Nothing ever seemed to go to time these days. Chasing their tails all day, Tomkin grumbled constantly.

The auction. They had talked it over endlessly, putting a top price on their own offer which varied from day to day. The Colonel had set his highest bid at £25,000; Lisa was sure the place was well worth £27,000 and Tomkin had opted for £28,000, insisting they would get far more than that for the house they lived in now. Tomkin thought it was worth more than £40,000. It was very well kept, an ideal family house.

Paddy Joe had no idea what either place could be worth. The old farmhouse had not been lived in for years and two of the barns were rotten; and there was no piped water or sewage pipes but the foundations were there, to build on afresh. And it was next door to Lisa's home, so the fences could be removed and the land run together.

24

The place had expanded since the Colonel went into partnership with Lisa. There were six brood bitches, two stud dogs, and now nine brood mares, as well as their foals. But prices for horses were falling all the time; foals went for so little that they weren't worth sending to market, yet, if they were kept, they ate their heads off; and money vanished, with prices higher and higher and no prospect of times getting better.

Lisa had four more mares at livery now. But that meant more and more work, and nobody seemed to have time for more than getting up, working and falling exhausted into bed. Paddy Joe helped before school and afterwards, when he had time; but with exams to pass and the need to get into university, he spent more and more time with his books, and even the dogs were not trained as well as before.

If they lived next door it would mean more time to spare as it now took half an hour from his place to Deep Hollow farm; and the Colonel had to be taken and fetched. He could no longer walk there, striding out like a young man. It took him hours to crawl, he commented irritably and his lack of strength angered him. He hated age; it made a mockery of a man. He would never admit that he could not keep up with Paddy Joe, who had learned to slow his pace and pretend that he was finding it hard to manage at the Colonel's speed. But he knew the Colonel wasn't fooled.

"Do you think we'll get it?" Paddy Joe asked.

"We're going to get it," Tomkin said. "By hook or by crook ... it's the only thing left to us, short of selling up; and can you imagine Lisa without her dogs and the old man without his horses?"

Tomkin had never referred to the Colonel as the old man before. Paddy Joe, busy scrubbing the pig stink out of Storm, paused and looked up at him.

"It's up to us from now on, Paddy Joe," Tomkin said. "He can't do as he did; and it's no use pretending."

"Supper," the Colonel said. He was standing watching them, and Paddy Joe wondered if he had heard them, but he gave no sign. He leaned on his stick, looking at Storm, who had given up struggling and was submitting to the hose.

"Those dogs will stink for days. You'd better find something to drown the smell if they're sleeping in your room tonight," the Colonel said, knowing very well that both would bark all night if left outside. They guarded too well, against moths and butterflies and cruising birds if left to themselves; indoors, they did sleep, as the sounds were all different. And they knew better than to wake Paddy Joe because a fox had cried to the moon. He could lean out of bed and shake them.

"First day of the summer holidays," Paddy Joe said. "Can I come to the auction?"

"If you promise not to sneeze or nod or wave a hand; I've no intention of bidding by accident," the Colonel said. He led the way indoors. The dogs were shut in, but would come to be fed later.

Darkness was shading the sky. The trees moved in a shiver of wind. Long shadows hid the garden. Paddy Joe, looking back, knew he didn't want to leave his

26

home. This was safety, and had been for all of his life, as long as he could remember; home where Grandee had looked after him, and Martha, her housekeeper. Martha too had died last year, falling gently asleep one evening in her room at the Home she had gone to live in when the Colonel bought the house.

She had left him her books; Paddy Joe had them on a shelf in his room, her old Sunday school prizes: *Robinson Crusoe*, and *Little Maid Marigold*, *Little Lord Fauntleroy* and *Misunderstood*. He had never read any of them. They were bound in red leather, edged with gold, with the prize cards pasted into them. They didn't look as if anyone had read them, not even Martha.

Later that night, his school books tidied away, his essay neatly written, Paddy Joe brought in the dogs and fed them. They came meekly, still abashed, knowing they had done wrong. They watched him anxiously, but he showed no sign of anger, so that Gale came to nudge his knee, and Storm leaned against him, mouth open, panting. His eyes laughed up at Paddy Joe. Storm, both the Colonel and Tomkin suspected, found human beings endearingly silly, and Tomkin, uncharacteristically, found himself looking at the big dog and wondering what it did think of them, if it thought at all. There were times when the dog's eyes were unnerving; as if he judged them all and found them sadly wanting in sense.

Paddy Joe sat on the window seat, listening to the night. Somewhere below a rustling betokened the old boar badger, rooting for food in the bushes.

Storm growled and Paddy Joe silenced him with a lifted hand. Gale jumped on to the seat and looked out. She was a dainty creature, slender, but with good bones and a rich black and gold coat. Her head was delicately made compared with Storm's, her expression totally feminine. Paddy Joe put an arm round her, and she settled against him as an owl flew past on shadowed wings, and whooped softly to his mate.

The moon hung low over the trees.

The dark held mystery.

Paddy Joe, watching, felt that somewhere out there was the key to the strange happenings in life; the reason for everything; the way to the future when he would be grown and know the truth about the world, and know how to deal with people, and would never make mistakes.

Below him he heard Tomkin coughing. On the other side of the wall, the Colonel shifted his aching body in his bed, wishing he were young, without adult cares; and beside Paddy Joe the two dogs watched, knowing only that they were safe and fed and cared for, and tomorrow would be as exciting as today.

Chapter Three

The morning of the auction sale dawned fine and blowy. A high wind raced through the trees, and the dogs, when let out to play, ran like fools, excited by the speeding invisible creature that tossed the branches and blustered in the grass and howled round the corner of the house.

There was only time to give the dogs a brief run; to move Shadowfax into the field, where he had water in his trough, and toss hay to him over the fence. Only time for a quick breakfast, the Colonel making instant coffee, Tomkin making toast, Paddy Joe putting plates and cups and saucers on the bench by the window. None of them troubled to sit down. Paddy Joe wandered round restively, plate in hand, watching the wind pack the clouds before it into towering dark peaks.

"Thunder before the end of the day and the auction's held outside," Tomkin said. The Colonel nodded absently, his mind on his throbbing toe. He leaned heavily on his stick as they walked out to the car.

Lisa and Debbie were already in the field. There was a big marquee, but the wind was playing havoc with it. One guy rope had already been torn from the ground, and the canvas shook as if great beasts were trapped inside.

"Dealers," Tomkin said in disgust, watching the sleek cars drive in to the rough car park. Paddy Joe watched the strangers congregate. They seemed to know one another and all were of a type. Solidly fleshed men with smooth faces, wearing sheepskin jackets, and all the women were blonde, made up, and older, on close inspection, than they seemed at first glance, all wearing smart clothes, all with the same cold eyes that measured those around them, and looked away, uninterested.

There were several local farmers. Moffat was there, an untidy man as fat as his biggest pig, his larded chins tucking down on to his chest, his eyes lost in rolls of fat, his vast legs corduroy clad. Beside him his wife stood, dwarfed, wearing a thin grey coat that she clutched round her as if it would defend her from the world.

Lisa, standing among them, was more beautiful than he had realised, Paddy Joe thought, turning to look at her, at her clean-boned face, at her sleek shining hair, at the warm brown eyes that smiled at him as she intercepted his glance. She was slender, elegant, in a dark blue trouser suit, a green jersey showing its roll neck above the lapels.

Paddy Joe wandered to the far end of the field. The house stood grim against the sky and he was uneasy; there was an odd feeling about it today, a brooding sullenness that made him turn his jacket collar up and want to get back among people again. He wished he could have brought the dogs. As he turned to go, he thought he heard, very soft and far away, the soft jangle of a muted bell, almost like a cowbell. He looked about him, but there was nothing to be seen, and though he listened, all was once more still, except for the shrieking wind that blew eddies of dust from the dirty paths. The boarded windows were inimical.

It was a horrible place. They could never work on it and make a home of it; they could never live there. Paddy Joe walked back to the marquee and went inside. He hadn't realised that there were other things to be auctioned. The long tables were covered with objects of all kinds. He wandered among them, bemused.

Where had such things come from? He couldn't imagine why anyone should want to keep the battered little child's high chair, let alone buy it.

"That's early Victorian," a woman said behind him. Paddy Joe recognised her. She lived on the next door farm. "And the bird cage is at least 150 years old. These things have been in store for years in my father's barns, to keep them safe. The pictures were on my walls. I hate them."

Paddy Joe stared at the bird cage. It was dingy with age and green with verdigris. Nobody would bid for that, nor for the broken model of a small ship of the line, of about Nelson's time; a modern model, Paddy Joe thought. He wandered on, finding a huge old sink with a lead base, vast enough to dip a sheep in; a weird contraption labelled Lot 59 that when he looked in the catalogue proved to be a Victorian fire fighting machine. He looked at it more closely; it was a water barrel on wheels, with a length of hose attached.

Debbie came over to him, grinning.

"Come and see what I've found," she said.

Paddy Joe followed her to a table covered in extraordinary objects; one of the oldest typewriters he had ever seen; a battered ancient camera on a stand with a black hood under which the photographer once lurked; a marble statue of a naked Roman, wearing nothing but his sword and helmet; the marble bust of a soldier, labelled in the catalogue "gentleman in uniform". At the end of the table were two pictures, so old and faded it was hard to make them out. One was of a pair of whippets, running in a field that had blended into the canvas, the other a still life, with a cabbage, two dead pheasants and an equally dead duck, with a huge cooking ladle beside it.

"Can't imagine anyone wanting *that*," Debbie said. "But there is one thing I rather like." She led the way to another picture, delicate and modern, of birds, painted on silk. "It's Chinese; it's lovely; and would go with my room."

Paddy Joe looked at it and thought he might bid for it, and give it to Debbie. It couldn't fetch more than a pound. He paused at a collection of birds' eggs in a cardboard shoe box. There were more than a hundred there; he identified thrush and black-bird, and then looked down at the tiny meticulous labels; osprey; peregrine; hobby. All the protected birds. Someone had collected them; it must be long ago. No one could do that now, without being fined heavily under the Wild Birds Protection Act.

"The house and land comes last," Tomkin said. "We can't go; they'll probably get rid of all this in a couple of hours. They work very fast. Whatever you do, watch yourself; we don't want a broken grand-father clock, or a pair of chapel doors."

Paddy Joe couldn't imagine anyone wanting a pair of chapel doors. He sat down on a hard seat that was far too small, as the auctioneer climbed on to the rostrum, which was made up of a box standing on an old kitchen table, and seemed remarkably unsafe.

The auctioneer was a small man, plump, grey haired, with a fine moustache that blew out in front of him as he talked. His sheepskin coat made him bulkier than he was, and the small bowler on the back of his head reminded Paddy Joe of Laurel and Hardy.

"A brass-rimmed nursery fender; very useful for the family man; in lovely condition, what am I bid?"

"Fifteen pounds, thank you sir, who'll give me sixteen, seventeen I'm bid, done for seventeen; thank you sir, twenty; twenty-one; done for twenty-one? Any advance on twenty-one. All done!" Down went the gavel on the table, and one of the stewards was walking across the room with a slip for the buyer to fill in name and address and Paddy Joe was staring bemusedly at what appeared to be a perfectly ordinary brass fender that had cost somebody twenty-one pounds.

"Victorian," the Colonel said. "Bought by a dealer, you'll see. Just watch that man, and see if he doesn't buy a whole lot more stuff; probably all the brass, and those copper pans."

Paddy Joe turned his head to see a tiny grey haired man in a dark coat with a fur collar that matched the fur hat that sat askew on his head. His eyes were masked behind dark glasses that hid his expression.

Debbie's Chinese picture was held up; the bidding started at twenty-five pounds, and Paddy Joe gave up. They would never get the house and land; they might as well go home. Gloom swept over him, and a slow anger at the thought of so much money in other people's hands to spend so incredibly. The picture went for £220; and then the bidding began for the two faded paintings, and even the Colonel listened incredulously as the price soared to £1,000, and then to £2,000, and the first picture finally went to a small gipsy-like woman in a red coat, a multicoloured headscarf and long dangling gold earrings, who bid £2,300.

"All done for £2,300 to the lady in the red coat."

"Somebody's done, I reckon," Tomkin said.

"It's signed," Lisa said. "I've never heard of the artist, but the pictures are by the same man; maybe she knows something we don't."

34

"And where have we got the money to bid on pictures?" the Colonel asked. He was glaring with a thunderous expression at a woman standing beside the collection of birds' eggs. She turned away uneasily, fingering her hair.

The second picture reached £2,800; the battered model boat went for £68; the little high chair for £58; a Victorian doll's pram for £200, and then came the birds' eggs.

"A very nice cardboard box, a specimen cardboard box," the auctioneer said.

"It just happens to have a collection of birds' eggs in it. Nobody would buy them today, and whoever buys the box will undoubtedly throw the eggs away. Now what am I bid for this beautiful little box?"

The box was sold for sixteen pounds.

"They're mad," Tomkin said, as a couple who were obviously father and son went forward to give their names and addresses.

"Here comes the Roman statue," Debbie said. "Just imagine waking up to see that every morning. It's horrible. Can you imagine anyone wanting it?"

It was soon very obvious that several people wanted it, and even the Colonel whistled when it was sold to a tall man wearing a grey suit piped with black, and a Robin Hood hat with a pheasant's feather stuck in the band, for £420.

"We might as well go home," Lisa said. "People are buying totally silly things at totally silly prices."

Paddy Joe could not sit still. The wind whistled round his legs and he was cold and he was restless. He went outside, and discovered another tent had been erected, where two ladies dispensed tea and sandwiches. The bread was fresh and the ham luscious. Paddy Joe bought three, and went down the field to eat them.

He stood with his back against a vast oak, watching the wind billow the tent, hearing the soft singsong voice of the auctioneer, the words inaudible, sounding like a litany. There were cars of all kinds drawn up in ranks on the grass, and the threatening clouds were lower, holding a promise of a drenching later on.

Cattle grazed in the field; beyond the fence Lisa's mares were standing quiet, while the foals galloped crazily. One of the dogs barked, its voice muted by distance, and the others started. Maybe there was a prowler, Paddy Joe thought, and vaulted the fence and ran.

There was no one around. He shared his last sandwich with the grey mare that Lisa loved, and returned to his stand under the tree. The wind had dropped for a moment; and once again he thought he heard a bell. It was an offkey, out of tune jangle, a teasing noise, on the edge of sound, but again there was nothing to account for it.

Debbie came to join him, walking swiftly, tired of sitting still.

"They've just sold a filthy old carpet for £800," she said. "What would you do with £800?"

Paddy Joe thought. There were a number of things he would do, but not one of them included buying a faded dirty carpet.

"It was Turkish," Debbie said.

"It's still daft," Paddy Joe was only half listening. The bell reminded him of something and he thought he heard the jangle again, but Debbie was already walking back to the tent, and he must be wrong. There was nothing here to account for the noise. It must come from the tent. Perhaps something was hung up on wires, and was jangling.

They were selling silver when he returned. Fifty pounds for a cream jug, and fifty pounds for a teapot; then he realised all the silver was going to one of the blonde women; her over-powdered face seemed to crack open as she bid.

There was another woman bidding, but each time she was forced to give up.

The Colonel limped off to find food and drink. He returned half an hour later.

"Crowd's thinning out, now the important stuff's gone," he said. "There aren't nearly so many cars in the car park. All the carpets, furniture and the pictures and silver are sold; what's left are the family cars, not the big Rovers and Daimlers. Dealers from London, all of them."

"Gives us a chance," Tomkin said. "Moffat's still here. Do you think he could be after it?"

"Where would he get the money?" Lisa asked.

Tomkin shrugged.

"Ways and means. Or he could be here for someone else."

There was a far away thunder rumble.

The auctioneer raised his voice. They were coming to the end of the catalogue. Paddy Joe worked out that he was selling one lot every two minutes; there

37

were six lots to go before the house and land. Any time now.

The last item, described in the catalogue as a small antique oak Welsh Cwbydd Daedarn, was sold for £815. Paddy Joe went to look at it; he couldn't imagine why it fetched so much, but then he didn't care for antiques anyway. He liked everything modern as tomorrow. The past was over; forgotten; he was impatient for the future.

"Now," Tomkin said, but the auctioneer was leaving the rostrum, settling his hat on his head, obviously intent on refreshments.

"Might as well go for another coffee ourselves," the Colonel said, easing his foot, guarding it against passers by who might knock it and flame pain into agony.

There was another man mounting the rostrum, a younger man, tall and dark, his scarlet shirt a flaunting brilliance muted by a wide black tie. His suit was palest gold and the Colonel snorted audibly, while Tomkin sat stony faced, as if unable to believe his eyes. The dark hair was sleek and shining and carefully waved.

"His perm must take hours," Debbie whispered, and giggled.

Paddy Joe eased his own jeanclad legs, expecting a soft voice to emerge from the peacock-clad frame, but the voice that did come was incredibly deep and held a hint of laughter in it.

He had a much slower way of speaking, without the dancing lilt that had characterised the older man. He warmed to his subject, waving a hand towards the ruined house that could be seen through the opening in the tent. Lightning flickered across the sky.

"Now we come to the important business of the day," he said. "This lovely old building, full of history; and twenty-eight acres of the finest grazing land in the county. There's a little to do on the house, but can't you see it? A gentleman's residence, standing nobly against the sky, the roof restored to its former glory, with spacious gardens, room for a tennis court and swimming pool; landscaped woods around the house, giving privacy. A dream of a home, for those with imagination and adventure in their souls."

"And a deep pocket," an anonymous voice said from somewhere near Paddy Joe.

"Who'll start the bidding at fifty thousand pounds?"

The Colonel seemed to shrink. Tomkin stared, and Paddy Joe was not sure whether he were glad or sorry that the price was so far beyond their reach. There was dead silence in the tent.

"Oh come, gentlemen. Make me an offer now; forty thousand pounds?"

There was no offer.

"Well then, what am I offered? Somebody must want this lovely place; it's the opportunity of a lifetime; it might make a hotel, or a country club; or a very successful small farm with lovely buildings. Come on, someone make an offer."

"Three thousand pounds," Tomkin said.

"Four thousand," Moffat said from behind them.

The Colonel glared.

"Four thousand, five hundred."

"Five," Moffat said.

"Six thousand," Tomkin waved his catalogue to make sure he had been seen and heard.

"Six thousand one hundred," Moffat said.

"It seems to be between you two gentlemen," the auctioneer said. "Come on, sir, surely you won't let him have it for such a paltry sum. Bid me six five."

"Six three," Tomkin said.

Lightning was flashing in the sky. Far away the thunder rolled, and Lisa and Debbie left hastily to put the horses in and quieten the dogs, and take indoors those that would be most frightened. Paddy Joe offered to join them, but Lisa shook her head.

"Stay on and then come and tell us what happened," she whispered, before running across the field to her own property. Both she and Debbie climbed the fence.

Thunder rumbled again.

The rain drumming on the tent drowned voices.

Tomkin was holding up his hand. Moffat was waving his programme. The auctioneer beckoned the two men to come closer to the rostrum. The Colonel was penned in, his foot throbbing, his mind on his pain, and only half on the bidding. He trusted Tomkin not to go too high. Paddy Joe crept along the row. There was only a handful of people left now, and the wind sighed under the chairs and benches, wafted papers and programmes and paper cups across the ground, as Tomkin held up his hand again.

Moffat shook his head.

"All done," the auctioneer yelled. "All done for twenty-eight thousand five hundred pounds."

"Holy mackerel." The Colonel was jerked back to the world again and stood, glaring at Tomkin. "The man's gone out of his mind. We said twenty-seven was our limit. We can't raise that amount of money right now."

"We can," Tomkin said. He braced himself to stare the Colonel in the eyes. "My money added to yours; I've got quite a bit put by. But I want a partnership; equal shares. We can get a loan till our house is sold."

The Colonel stared at him.

Paddy Joe suddenly realised his guardian was a very old man; the white hair was thin; the blue eyes pathetic, in a face now lined and wrinkled, above an old tortoise neck. It seemed to have happened overnight, yet Paddy Joe knew he had never really thought about his guardian before.

The Colonel nodded.

Wearily he stumbled to the car, not looking back. Paddy Joe wondered if he ought to help the old man, but Tomkin put his hand on the boy's arm.

"He's better on his own," Tomkin said. "The day we have to help him, he'll give up. Leave him his pride. I've just knocked it; let it grow again."

There was a break in the clouds. Tomkin walked across the field to look at the old house. The last rain fell on it, a rainbow shining behind it as a pale sun tried to thrust its way through the dense sky cover. Paddy Joe trailed behind, wishing he too could add money to the partnership.

"I can't do anything," he said forlornly.

"Most of your grandmother's house belongs to you, Paddy Joe," Tomkin said. "The Colonel hadn't enough capital to buy it when your grandmother died; there's a deed in the bank made out in your joint names. Half the money at least is yours; probably more. I don't know. So you'll have a major share in this; it's our house, all three of us, this time. I've never had a stake in anything before. I've been saving all my life, in the hope that one day ..."

Paddy Joe looked at their new acquisition, at the grim brick walls, and the boarded windows; at the derelict barns and the fields filled with nettles and thistles, except for the one field that was still being grazed. There were ten black bullocks there, now dragging at hay which had been spread for them to supplement the thin grass. It had been a wet summer and the hooves had churned the field to mud.

"We're mad," he said.

"Maybe." Tomkin turned back to the car. "You go and tell Lisa. Stay to tea if you're asked. I'd like a little while alone with the old man. Make him feel part of the world again. He's desolate, only just realising that he needs us now more than we need him. Old age is cruel, Paddy Joe. Just you remember that when my turn comes; be kind."

"Were you kind?" Paddy Joe asked.

"There's no way to soften it," Tomkin said. "Get off, lad. Lisa needs help."

Paddy Joe did not look back. Tomkin watched him walk across the fields, envious of Paddy Joe's youth;

jealous for a moment of his future. Then he set his jaw and turned towards the car.

Paddy Joe stopped at the fence.

Again he was sure he could hear the sound of a bell. The teasing jangle mocked him for a moment, as if some cow had moved her head, and paused to graze.

But none of the cattle were belled.

Maybe there was a piece of metal blowing in the wind in the old house. On an impulse he walked in through the front door, which hung on one hinge, and sagged to the dirty ground. Tramps had slept in the ground floor rooms. There were the memories of old fires, the ashes long cold; a damp and smelly mattress, empty tins, hacked open roughly by a knife. There was the promise of long hours of sheer slavery; of weeks before the place was even halfway habitable; Tomkin was crazy. He had thrown their money away. The Colonel was right and the whole thing was impossible.

Again came the tinny jangle of the bell.

Paddy Joe searched the floor and the upstairs rooms, but there was nothing to give even a hint of such a noise.

He stood outside, listening.

Nothing moved. The sky had cleared, the clouds torn to rags, flying away on the wind. The wind itself had dropped. The meadow was wet from rain. The cattle moved slowly, content. A magpie passed. One for sorrow. Its mate followed. Two for a joy. A third came after. Paddy Joe couldn't remember the rest of the rhyme, but at least it meant something more

43

cheerful than sorrow. Was it three for silver?

He vaulted the fence and ran towards Deep Hollow, coming into the kitchen to find Lisa had made tea for him as well.

"Tomkin got it. For twenty-eight thousand five hundred pounds," Paddy Joe said. Lisa stared at him.

"Dear Heaven, he's mad. I don't know why we ever agreed to such a crazy scheme."

Paddy Joe sat down at the table, and discovered he had no appetite. The food almost choked him. A year ago, he wouldn't have cared. Now, he understood so much more; and he didn't like the things he understood.

Chapter Four

He helped Debbie with the horses, but Debbie's mind was not on her work, and she was not inclined to talk. Paddy Joe grew more and more irritable, and when she left him on his own and vanished into the house, he wanted to lash out at someone, anyone, because nothing was ever the way he hoped.

Debbie was only a few moments inside; and then at the front of the house, a car hooted, and the front door slammed. He heard her quick feet on the drive, heard the revving engine, and then the sounds died.

Lisa came out to finish Debbie's work. She glanced at Paddy Joe and decided on silence. But he was easier with her; they worked companionably and by the time they had finished he was relaxed, and ready to go indoors and drink coffee and look at the new pups, born the night before, in the warm room behind the big kitchen where Lisa always whelped her bitches. There was a whelping kennel outside, but here there was a sofa to lie on, and no fear of cold winds to chill newborn pups, or a wearying bitch.

"Nine names to find, Paddy Joe," Lisa said.

"Lunacy; Tomfoolery; Bankruptcy," Paddy Joe said. "Lisa, Tomkin's crazy; have you looked at that place?"

"Daily, for years," Lisa said. "I thought of one possibility. I was told of someone who has one of those big caravans for sale, you know, the double affairs, with several rooms. It's not in its first youth, but it would be more comfortable than the stable flat and the Colonel wouldn't have stairs to climb. It's going cheaply; somebody emigrating. I thought of having it here to make a holiday place, to let in the summer. That would add income too. The place would make a base for you three to start with. We'll need the money from that house quickly; we'll have to borrow to buy Tomkin's Folly."

It was named already, if not in fact, in their minds. Paddy Joe made a detour across the land on the way home, looking at the gaunt walls standing ghostly under the moon. Beyond them was a huge tree, its spreading branches shadowing the ground. Paddy Joe walked towards it. It must have been hundreds of years old; a great beech tree, its leaves shivering in a breeze that chilled him.

He stood beneath it, looking up, and from immediately above him came again the jangle of a bell.

He began to climb.

46

It was not easy in the dark, and the bell sounds increased, as if something were trapped up there, and becoming angry. He swung himself to a branch half-way up the tree and then ducking his head too swiftly he banged it on the branch beyond him. An angry beak swept towards his eyes.

He remembered the peregrine falcon he had seen flying above him.

This bird was caught by its jesses. The leather thongs were dangling, fixed firmly on the branch on which the bird had perched. It must have flapped in terror, swung, and righted itself. He would need help to free it, but it could not stay there, a prisoner, to die of starvation.

He climbed down the tree and ran all the way home, arriving out of breath, just as Tomkin was shutting the dogs away.

"You never do anything round here these days," Tomkin said angrily. "Out till all hours, with Debbie I suppose."

He hadn't meant to say it and he wished he hadn't said it.

"Debbie was out," Paddy Joe said. "I helped Lisa do Debbie's jobs."

He remembered the falcon.

"There's a peregrine trapped in the beech tree at Cockshoot's."

"Can't do anything at this time of night. Too dangerous," Tomkin said. "We'll go at first light. If it frees itself, good. If not, it won't come to harm if we leave it another few hours."

"It needs food," Paddy Joe said.

47

"There's meat. Can you get it to it without killing yourself?"

It was a ridiculous question. Paddy Joe took the meat and went out into the dark. The dogs heard him and howled, wanting to go with him. The moon had gone. It was too dark to climb, but he set his teeth and went up, by guess work, using his hands and feet to tell him where there were footholds and handgrips, knowing he was being stupid, that Tomkin would be furious if he knew, but he wanted to feed the bird, somehow.

He could hear the jingle, increasing; he was close. He looked up, seeing the bulk of the bird on the branch, the sky paler than the tree and the falcon. He eased the meat upwards and the bird stabbed at it, taking it from him. It had not fed for three days. Hunger overcame fear.

Paddy Joe climbed down, and went to bed, satisfied. The dogs were both waiting for him in his room. Tomkin had taken them up for him. There was a tray on the bedside table. Cocoa in a flask and sandwiches, and scones. Tomkin was apologising. There was cheese in one of the sandwiches. Paddy Joe shared it with the dogs who sat in front of him watching every mouthful, a pool of saliva collecting at their paws.

He set the alarm for first light, and went to bed, to fall asleep at once and dream he was climbing endlessly into the sky, trying to reach a bird that eluded him, flapping from branch to branch, just as he put out a hand to grasp it.

He felt as if he had not slept at all when the

alarm clock rang. The day was just beginning, the first light grey over the trees, the dew wet on the grass, a hint of sun in the east. He made coffee and sliced bread for toast and had food ready when Tomkin came down, looking as if he too had not slept.

"Got cold feet over that house," Tomkin said. "Don't tell the Colonel."

"We'll do it," Paddy Joe said, turning comforter for once. He thought back to the day before, feeling older, and responsible now for both Tomkin and the Colonel. He would have to do more for them; the Colonel was doing less and that made more work for Tomkin.

"Putting the house on the market today," Tomkin said. "It'll be a wrench, leaving it. We've had some good times here."

Paddy Joe had grown up here; first with his grand-mother, Grandee, and then with the Colonel and Tomkin; they had taught him to fish and to shoot; Tomkin had taught him about animals, taking him out at night to watch badgers, or out in the early dawn to stalk deer; taking him camping in the rough parts of Scotland where the Colonel fished and Paddy Joe watched ospreys diving and catching their own fish; more expert than any human. They had found birds' nests, noting them, leaving the eggs untouched, never disturbing the birds.

"Let's get that bird."

Paddy Joe had his leather gauntlets with him; and Tomkin brought a sack. They expected trouble.

There was no one yet about. The morning was noisy with birdsong, and two rabbits loped across the field beside them, at the far corner of the hedge, then spotted them and were away, white scuts bobbing. A hare groomed itself on a little mound, squeezing both ears between its front paws; then caught their scent on the wind and followed the rabbits. A squirrel hissed at them from the hedge.

The falcon was caught almost at the end of a branch. He had little room for movement. He edged irritably, within a scope of a few inches. Tomkin looked up.

"Take both of us," he said.

Paddy Joe nodded. One to climb over the bird, the other below the bird; the one above to drop the sack over it. It would struggle. And they'd have to cut the jesses.

"Whoever lost it is a fool," Tomkin said. "So likely it's not been properly manned. And likely it will fight us. Need to watch your eyes."

Paddy Joe began to climb. The bell jangled angrily. The bird could see him plainly now, and fear mastered it. It had been caught only a few short weeks before, caught illegally, and hidden in a back shed. Freedom had come through an incautious movement, and it had flown away, into the open sky, but the sound of its bell haunted it, and the thongs round its feet trailed irritatingly, and, when it had landed to rest, they had caught tenaciously, holding it more firmly than it had ever been held on the rough block on which its captor had kept it.

Its first owner had been a boy no older than Paddy Joe.

The bird did not trust boys.

50

It stabbed downwards with its beak, but Paddy Joe was out of reach, climbing swiftly, his eye on the branch above the bird.

Tomkin came slowly, wishing he were younger. The tree was difficult for him but he would never admit that. Where Paddy Joe could go, he would go. He eased himself on to the crutch of a branch and sat for a moment, panting.

Above him, Paddy Joe looked out across the fields; at the Cockshoot house, standing in ruins beyond him. On the far side of the wall he saw movement, and a moment later Moffat came round the corner, measuring the length of wall beside the tree.

Paddy Joe hissed softly and Tomkin looked up.

Paddy Joe pointed.

Tomkin turned his head, staring, wondering what on earth the man thought he was doing. But better to wait and see, and not, for the moment, yell to him that he was trespassing. Moffat wrote something in a notebook and disappeared round the corner.

Paddy Joe climbed on.

The bird was firmly caught, which was as well, as they had no net, and no other means of ensuring that they could trap it. Only the sack. It was tucked inside his anorak. Once above the bird, he paused. It looked enormous; its yellow eye watched him, inimical. The beak could strike. The bird could move in a small circle, swaying towards him.

He angled himself and dropped the sack over it, surprising it. Tomkin was ready below to fasten the neck, to cut the encircling thongs, to swathe the fierce talons, in swift movements come from long remembered practice. He had once owned a hawk.

He held it, while Paddy Joe climbed down. It would be dangerous to hold the bird and climb at the same time. Tomkin had a long line that he fastened to the throat of the sack. He held on to the branches with one hand and lowered the bird to Paddy Joe.

The bell jangled contemptuously.

"We'll have to make a hood," Tomkin said. "You can buy some leather. Long time since I made one; I hope I remember how."

He made a perch inside the shed; a big block of wood, placed on the bench. He made a temporary pair of jesses, and put them on the bird's legs, then leashed it, and fastened it firmly. He put meat on the block, and removed the sack. The bird thrashed its wing, fanning the air in terror.

"Leave it alone for now," Tomkin said. "Later, we'll hood him. He's been half tamed. Give him time to recover."

They left the bird in the shed. Tomkin fastened an old piece of corrugated asbestos against the window, to give him darkness, and then went indoors. Paddy Joe followed, and began cooking the bacon.

"Where on earth have you two been?" the Colonel asked testily, coming into the kitchen in dressing gown and slippers, his white hair brushed in an untidy quiff that gave him the look of an irritable heron.

"Catching a hawk," Paddy Joe said.

"There's no need to be funny." The Colonel glared at him.

"True as I stand here," Tomkin said. "He was caught by his jesses in the big tree beyond Cockshoot's."

"I'm selling that place," the Colonel said. "We were mad to buy it. Moffat was there this morning, measuring; he wants to convert the old place into a pig farm; he's coming back tonight for my final answer."

"No," said Tomkin and Paddy Joe together.

"Lisa's getting one of the big caravans for us to live in till it's done," Paddy Joe said; "It'll be plenty big enough for the three of us. We can sleep in the field and work every hour we're free. It won't take long, you'll see."

"It'll take longer than I've got," the Colonel said. "I won't live to see it finished. It will take years." He was suddenly silent. Paddy Joe looked at Tomkin, who spoke softly. "We've all got years." The Colonel did not hear.

The old man was standing by the window, lost in his own thoughts.

"Dogs, cats, they're for keeping as pets," he said. "A hawk, no. It's a wild bird, born free. It goes free, Paddy Joe."

"It's starving, terrified, and injured," Tomkin said. "We nurse it back to health first. It couldn't even hunt. It's been banging its wings against branches all night and all day; for twenty-four hours, I reckon. It's in a bad way."

"This isn't a home for sick animals," the Colonel said. "You're as bad as Paddy Joe. If he had his way we'd be full up with dogs and cats and other

53

strays. It's got to stop. Money doesn't stretch, not these days."

He went out, to dress, blundering angrily upstairs over their heads. Twenty minutes later he took the car out of the garage and drove away.

"And he shouldn't be driving either," Tomkin said. "Awkward as a dog with a splinter in his paw."

Paddy Joe was eating toast, talking excitedly about the falcon. Paddy Joe had always wanted a hawk, had read every book he could find on hawks, had dreamed of owning his bird, taking it on his fist, flying it above him, soaring in the sky and then calling it down to his lure, the bird tame and coming to him because he wanted it, and the bird wanted him.

"It will have to go free, Paddy Joe," Tomkin said, knowing where the boy's thoughts led him. "Don't make plans. Not for a hawk of your own."

"I can tame it," Paddy Joe said.

"And is that wise? It has come to harm through man; it should never trust man. Remember the pheasant you tamed?"

Paddy Joe did remember. The bird had come to be handfed every day; until one day a lad with a gun saw it and killed it as it stood, taking crumbs from the lawn. Now they clapped their hands to scare the birds away, teaching them to fly from man. Taking a bird on the wing was one thing; hitting a tame bird was another altogether.

"You can go over to Horton and find out the price of bricks for me, Paddy Joe," Tomkin said. "A ride will do you good. Time you had exercise."

"And Shadowfax," Paddy Joe said.

"He's still too lame. Vet's coming over again to look at that leg. You can take your bike. That doesn't need a vet if you do something stupid on it."

Tomkin was thinking of the vet's bills; not of Paddy Joe. It was useless to try and argue. Tomkin was always right.

Paddy Joe wheeled out his old bicycle. It was a fine morning, the sun bright, small clouds building in a blue sky, promising rain later. The dogs had been left at home. Their howls followed Paddy Joe along the lane.

The price of bricks made Paddy Joe stare. How many bricks would they need? And wood for beams and slates and tiles; even nails cost money and there would be a need for hundreds of nails.

Paddy Joe wrote the prices down in a notebook that Tomkin had given him. He mounted his bicycle again and rode down the street. The clouds were denser now and the wind was niggling. Tomkin had given him bread and cheese, and he stopped to eat in the lee of a wall.

A head poked over the wall, nudging Paddy Joe on the shoulder. He turned his head, glancing over the wall, and gasped.

The pony's coat was marked with blood. Great scabs disfigured his shoulders and his flanks. He was a tiny Shetland, but even then he must have been too young to leave his dam. There were bare patches on his withers and his neck was raw where a halter had cut into it. Mane and tail were a mass of matted hair, and flies teased at his eyes, feeding on the discharge that came from them.

The field beyond was a morass of mud.

Paddy Joe jumped the wall. The pony came to him and leaned against him, needing comfort.

Paddy Joe examined it, anger building.

He jumped the wall again, leaving the little beast forlorn, staring after him, his head drooping, and his small body dropped to the ground.

Tomkin was not at home; Paddy Joe went for Lisa, who listened and got out her car. They drove back through the town, and Paddy Joe took her to the wall. She had pony nuts in her hand, and held them out to the little animal.

"I'll see Moffat," she said. She was shaking with anger.

Paddy Joe never heard what happened. There had been raised voices and shouting, but Lisa came out, her head held high, and Paddy Joe saw the dirty curtain twitch.

"I'll get the horse box," Lisa said.

Tomkin was working at the kennels when they reached Deep Hollow. He listened to them, and went at once to couple the trailer to the old Land Rover. Within minutes they were jogging back down the lane for the third time. The day had gone, and nothing had yet been done. They would have to work late into the evening.

"Work all night," Tomkin said, when he saw the pony. "You ought to report him."

"He says he rescued it. Only had it two days and was getting the vet out tomorrow. It fell in the wagon and was trampled on by the other ponies."

56

"It's going to be a miracle if we keep him alive," Tomkin said. "What did you pay for him, Lisa?"

"Forty pounds," Lisa said. "Moffat said he cost him eighty."

"I'll be surprised if he cost him a fiver," Tomkin said, leading the tiny pony to the gate. "He's still got the auction lot number on his rump. In that condition...."

The pony was too weak to protest. He dropped on the straw, watching them as Tomkin drove. Paddy Joe got in beside him, stroking the mucky fur, and the pony put his head on Paddy Joe's knees, loving the fussing and the contact. He had been very lonely in the empty field. No one had been near him since the auction and before that there had only been fear; fear of the bigger ponies thrusting and heaving against him; fear of the shouting men who handled him roughly; fear of the jolting wagon and the noises of invisible monsters that surrounded him.

And then there had been the auction and the pen in which he had been crowded with other ponies and men poking and prodding at him, looking at him in disgust.

"The last auction was nearly a month ago," Paddy Joe said suddenly.

No one had even bothered to take the label off the pony.

"You can get him clean," Tomkin said. "Put him in the stall next to Shadowfax. That horse is kind and friendly and won't frighten him. He needs reassuring; it's a wonder he's so gentle."

"He's only a baby," Lisa said. She was still angry

and went to work on the yard with a hose and broom and a savagery that startled even Tomkin.

Paddy Joe worked on the pony. He cleaned and bathed his eyes, and cleaned his nose, which was also running. He wiped him down with soft cloths and smothered him in flea powder. The tangled mane and tail almost defeated him.

By the time the vet came he was at least clean and there was some semblance of order in the long hairs at neck and rump.

The vet whistled when he saw him.

"He's not old enough to leave his mother; and just look at him. What in heaven's name gets into people? He's going to need a lot of treatment, and even then ... maybe you'd best put him down."

"He's having a life here," Lisa said. "I don't care what it costs. Poor little devil."

"He looks very doubtful of all of this," Debbie said, putting out her hand to stroke the pony, who moved his head away, wanting to be alone and sleep, feeling his legs buckle under him.

"Doubting Thomas," Chris said. "We'll call him Thomas. So you'd better get used to us and to your name, lad."

The Colonel drove into the yard as the vet drove out.

"Now what?" he asked acidly, easing his throbbing foot from the car, and standing on it carefully, leaning on the wall.

"You shouldn't have driven," Tomkin said.

"I'll do as I choose. I'm not ninety yet. What was that visit for?"

Paddy Joe looked at his guardian. Not so long ago he had had to look up. Now they were eye to eye, and in a year Paddy Joe would look down.

"I asked a question," the Colonel said. Gout always made him irritable and impatient. "Is nobody going to answer it? Is there a conspiracy or something? Is one of the horses dead?"

"Come and look," Lisa said.

The Colonel followed her. Thomas was lying in his stall, hidden by darkness. Lisa switched on the light, revealing the bald patches and the suppurating sores, and the clouded eyes, and the pony, seeing people, tried to struggle to his hooves and stand.

The Colonel was at a total loss for words. He had never seen an animal in such a condition.

"Moffat had bought it at an auction for his children," Lisa said. "I talked him into selling it to me."

The Colonel turned to look at her. He guessed how the transaction had gone. Faced with a maltreated animal he would rather meet a man-eating tiger than Lisa. She looked a mild woman, but her anger was terrifying. Moffat would have had by far the worst of that encounter.

"This place is turning into a madhouse," the Colonel said. "We buy a place that isn't worth ten-pence, for a fortune; Paddy Joe brings home a falcon; and now we have a rescued pony. Will some-one tell me how this is going to repair our damaged fortunes?"

"We can sell the pony when he's fit," Lisa said.

"We keep him." The Colonel wasn't risking

another bad owner for a pony in such poor case, and Lisa knew it perfectly well.

"There's another risk to that pony," Tomkin said. "He's coughing. Suppose he's got flu? And all our horses at risk?"

It wasn't a happy thought.

Later that night Lisa made a barley mash and Paddy Joe fed it to the pony. He was ravenous and took it all.

"Maybe it isn't flu," Tomkin said, watching through the stable door. "But we're not out of the wood with him yet."

Shadowfax was watching over the partition. The pony looked up at the big horse, deriving comfort from another of his own kind nearby. Paddy Joe bolted the stable and padlocked the door, wondering what he would find in the morning. He was longing for bed. The dogs were done, and he could go home.

But at home there were two dogs who had been shut in for most of the day, impatient for a romp and a walk, and for food.

And the falcon needed feeding too. Tomkin had made the hood. It hid his face from the world and hid the world from him. Paddy Joe spoke softly as he went into the shed and put a lump of raw rabbit that Jake had given him, down on the perch beside him. The smell roused him. He took the meat in his talons and fed. Paddy Joe stroked the soft breast with a feather. The bird bore it quietly, at peace after eating. He left him on the block, wondering if he remembered freedom and hankered for it, or if he sat there, patient, his mind quite blank till Paddy Joe brought food. He was used to people; half tamed.

Paddy Joe went to sleep, and woke when Gale growled a warning and then Storm barked. He looked from the window, and wondered if he really saw the shadow of a man move along the fence.

Tomkin had woken too when the dogs barked. He looked from the window, uneasy. A voice spoke from the darkness.

"You've crossed me too often. Watch out." There was a laugh, and Moffat reeled on to the drive and shook a fist at Tomkin.

The man was drunk. Stupidity spoke when the beer was in, but for all that Tomkin was uneasy. Moffat had a reputation for malice and he had a brood of unruly sons. And Lisa had a way of stinging with her words.

Paddy Joe was soon asleep, but it was hours before Tomkin was able to forget the awkward world.

Chapter Five

Suddenly, there was so much to do that Paddy Joe never had time to stop and think, and even Tomkin was so busy that he forgot his worries about Moffat. They measured and worked out sums; calculated quantities of bricks and slates, and wood for beams and joists; they discussed flooring. The Colonel found a dealer with second-hand materials; bricks from condemned houses, some of them usable again. But they had to buy whole lots and sort them. Lorries came and dumped them, and whenever there was a free hour, everyone available helped to pick out the good bricks and make a dump of the useless broken pieces.

He made time for the falcon.

Khan fascinated him. The bird was regal, a lordly creature, with his own ways; he bowed to no man. Sometimes he came off the block willingly, hopping to Paddy Joe's gloved fist and standing silent, his brown eyes watchful. The mottling on his feathers was vivid; he longed to fly but his bruised wings hurt. He lifted them and lowered them, fanning Paddy Joe with the movement. The span was incredible.

He needed attention, all the time; so that soon everyone became used to seeing Paddy Joe, when he was not busy around the place, with Khan on his fist.

"Talk to him, endlessly," Tomkin said. The human voice was a training aid for dog and bird alike; a soothing sound, taming fear; a gentle sound, bringing reassurance. It was wise to avoid sharp notes; to speak in a semi-whisper, to recite, endlessly. Poems learned long ago, nursery rhymes, long speeches from Shakespeare, so that the bird listened, turning his head, staring up at his rescuer.

Kipling went down well, with a thumping rhythm that came strongly through each line, which seemed to fascinate the bird. Paddy Joe recited tags and couplets, digging hard in his memory. Gentle him; feed him; and slowly the pride grew, and a longing to send his bird flying high above him, into the open sky; to watch him soar against the sun, and plunge towards the lure. But first he must learn to trust.

Tickle him with a gentle feather. The bird stood, preening, but still; if startled, he flew on the fist and hung upside down, screaming, all his kingly presence gone, a frightened creature that needed to be stood again and soothed again, and reassured again.

Khan hated the whinny that greeted Paddy Joe

when he returned to the yard and Shadowfax saw him; at once he hung, and screeched, and Paddy Joe began to think this must be jealousy, a desire to gain attention for himself, so that Shadowfax too became resentful and his whickering sounded long before Paddy Joe reached home. The horse heard footsteps; knew always when his master was near, and he felt neglected, not aware that his leg needed resting. He became edgy and irritable when groomed; and after his grooming when Paddy Joe took the bird on his fist again. Khan was edgy too, dancing and bating, hanging and screaming, an unnerving, angry, ear splitting noise that Paddy Joe could not stand, and that drove the Colonel to constant protest.

It wasn't much fun.

Tomkin alone remained unmoved by the noise. He had tamed hawks before; and tamed a young fox and a badger cub. He was good with nervy young colts, and good too with growing lads, though that Paddy Joe did not realise.

"Go easy on him, Paddy Joe," Tomkin said, one bright morning when Khan was longing to fly and would not settle; when he hung and screamed and twice stabbed upwards with an angry beak, heavier than seemed possible; rage glittered in his eyes. The sky called him, and the lure of the hunt, and the need to fly; to wing powerfully upwards and away, to ride the air streams, to rid himself of the remorseless energy building in his body. He was almost fit.

"He'll go sour on us if he doesn't fly soon," Tomkin said. "We'll have to risk him, Paddy Joe.

64

He reminds me of one of your Kipling rhymes and I bet it's one you don't know."

"Bet you I do," Paddy Joe said.

"You clean out the stable tonight if you lose," Tomkin said. He grinned. He was sure he was on to a winner.

"Stopped in the straight when the race was his own—
Look at him cutting it – cur to the bone!"

The Colonel, coming into the room, took up the poem.

"Ask ere the youngster be rated and chidden
What did he carry and how was he ridden?"

Paddy Joe, settling Khan on his fist again, grinned in his turn. He finished the rhyme for them.

"Maybe they used him too much at the start.
Maybe Fate's weight-cloth is breaking his heart."

Tomkin laughed.

"OK. I lose. But it's worth it; remember, never overtrain; not a horse, or a dog, or a hawk."

"Or a boy," Paddy Joe said. Lighthearted again, he put Khan on his block, food beside him, and willingly went to help with the stable chores. Shadowfax, pleased to be noticed, butted and pushed and little Thomas nibbled three buttons from Paddy Joe's shirt before he even noticed.

Outside in the shed Khan slept and dreamed of a wide sky and a free fall and swift wings beating, while a bright sun shone overhead.

The long summer holiday always stretched endless, especially for those unable to go away. Paddy Joe, meeting one of his classmates in the village when shopping for stamps, mentioned the house they were renovating.

"Destroying, at the moment," he added ruefully. All the old wood was rotten, and had to come out; window frames, doors and door frames; the roof timbers that remained would have to be shifted. They would employ professionals for that; it wasn't a job for amateurs.

The word spread.

By the end of the week a team had formed under Tomkin, six boys and three girls from the school, all delighted to find something to do.

Tomkin set them to sorting bricks, a job that was harder on the hands than the girls had expected, but they set to with a will. The pile of discards grew; but so did the stack of usable bricks.

"The old colour," Tomkin said. He handled one of them almost lovingly. "Rich and warm in the sun, not like the modern reds; they lack the deep colours you get in these. See the old house restored, with ivy and creeper up the wall, standing in the late sun."

Even the Colonel was caught up in the planning and the arguing. They would restore the shell of the house, trying to keep the old shape and alter nothing; it had once been well proportioned, with beautiful rooms inside.

Inside, they would make new rooms; larger rooms; but how many? and for what? The Colonel wanted a study; Tomkin wanted his own sitting room and bedroom, and thought that Paddy Joe should have the same.

"Time to grow up," he said. "You won't be away

from us yet, not if you want to be a vet. Another year of school; six years of college; seven more years before you fly, Paddy Joe."

"If there's money for college," the Colonel said morosely, thinking of prices that rose all the time; of the cost of the building; of the fact that as yet they had no buyer for their own home; and money borrowed from the bank to pay for the old Cockshoot's house was eating away into their savings, taking interest all the time.

Paddy Joe sat up late that night, looking out of his bedroom window. The two dogs sat beside him, sniffing the night. They knew there was a hare at the end of the garden, a hedgehog, blundering invisibly through the bushes, a fox far away, calling to another fox, a barking dog in the distance, crying because it was left alone.

Paddy Joe knew none of this. Neither his ears nor his eyes nor his nose were sensitive enough. He only knew that shadows lay across the lawn, that the moon flitted in and out of cloud, that the trees rustled in a breeze that was a forerunner of a gale.

He had too much to think about. He had to plan. He wanted to be a vet more than he wanted anything in the world and had been working to that end ever since he met the Mableys, enthralled by the dogs and horses, fascinated by the various ailments, helping to dose a horse with lugworm, or to hold a pony while the vet treated it for a leg injury or an infection, being allowed, under supervision, to give the dogs their injections. That couldn't be wasted.

And now he had two invalids of his own. The

falcon had a damaged wing; it was not yet strong enough for flight; and there was Thomas. Thomas who was not yet responding to treatment; but who loved to run his head against Paddy Joe's shoulder while his sores were being bathed, and who, in his brighter moments, tried to nibble buttons from coat or shirt, so that Paddy Joe had learned to wear something closefitting and buttonless when he saw Thomas, whose needs took up a great deal of time.

Tomkin, looking over the stable door, would watch Paddy Joe dress the septic places, and bathe the weals on the pony's back, and knew he had a lever to deal with Moffat if the man became awkward. He asked the vet to make detailed notes about the pony's condition. Those would be sent to the RSPCA if there was trouble. And somehow, Tomkin was pretty sure there would be trouble, though he could not guess how it would come.

It was Debbie who discovered Thomas had a passion for toffee apples. She loved them and was standing eating one, while Paddy Joe combed out the pony's mane and tail, which now at least were free of tangles, but not yet shining with health. Thomas reached out his head and neatly snitched her titbit, leaving only the stick in her hand. He ate it with relish. After that Chris made a point of bringing him one every day. Chris loved making toffee apples, loved the sticky mess he produced and hated cleaning up the pan so that he was always grumbled at by someone.

Now, sitting alone in his room at night, his knees under his chin and his arms curled round them, hands interlocked, Paddy Joe remembered Debbie's fury that first evening and grinned to himself. Debbie had wanted the pan for potatoes for supper and found it not only sticky but burnt.

He had heard the quarrel in the stables, and Chris had come out some minutes later, irritable and edgy, feeling that everyone got at him all the time and it wasn't fair. Paddy Joe had been unsympathetic, as he had had to clean Chris's pan the night before. Time Chris began to grow up, Paddy Joe thought, from his superior status of being two years older.

College. It all came back to that. He didn't want the sort of job he could get straight from school; didn't want to spend his days in an office, or a factory, or in any way that meant being away from animals. Suppose he took a job as a stable lad at a racing stables? Could he save enough to stake him for six years? He doubted it. Tomkin had said the pay was bad.

So he had to earn all he could now; had to have money somehow, had to save and save and save.

He could not think of a way of earning anything; not in the amounts he needed. He went to bed, but could not sleep for once. He was hot and the dogs were restless, Storm twice padding to the window to put his paws on the sill and growl; Gale coming for comfort, pushing her nose at Paddy Joe, needing reassurance. They were too busy and the dogs were shut in more than usual. No one had time to watch them while they were on the building site. And an unwatched dog could be a nuisance, running off, or

running wild, or chasing somebody who raced un- •
expectedly into view. Too many people grew up
without animals and did not realise that a wise man
never runs in front of a strange dog; the dog will give
chase, his instincts overriding his training. Even the
best trained dog will run after a running cat. The
wise cats crouched against the ground, never moving.
Some cats never learned. Mad Cat knew you didn't
run from dogs, but Awful teased them, provoking
them to chase. And neither Storm nor Gale could
be called off rabbit or hare if they saw it first;
they were gone and deaf and blind to all calls.
Though if Paddy Joe saw the beast and told them
to stay, they stayed.

He slept at last and woke up tired and irritable,
coming down late, annoying the Colonel who
expected army habits.

"Early to bed, early to rise," the Colonel said, pre-
dictably. "What were you doing last night? You and
the dogs were bumbling around till all hours."

The Colonel slept downstairs since his stroke. It was
easier than dragging himself up to his room, and the
little room he had once used as a gunroom, where
he kept his guns and fishing tackle, now had a
camp bed in it.

"Thinking about ways of making money," Paddy
Joe said, intent on bacon and eggs.

The Colonel raised bushy white eyebrows and
Tomkin stopped with his fork midway to his mouth
and stared at Paddy Joe.

"Did you come by any?" he asked.

Paddy Joe shook his head.

"Not in the amount I need," he said.

"What are you planning to do?" the Colonel asked.

"Be a vet," Paddy Joe said, and left his chair and went out to see to the dogs, and then cycle over to treat Thomas, to avoid further discussion.

Behind him Tomkin and the Colonel looked at one another.

The Colonel sighed.

"I don't know whether it's better to be born knowing what you want to do, or not," he said. "Too many square pegs...."

"We have to find a way," Tomkin said. "Cockshoot's may not cost as much as we think. That second-hand stuff is working out very reasonably and there's more to be recovered than I expected. Jake's heard of another house that's being pulled down. We might get wood and doors from that."

"So long as it's not wormy or rotten," the Colonel said. He went to his room and sat for a long time looking at his account books. Later that day someone was coming to look at their house. If the agent was right, and they could get the price they were asking; and if they could pick up more second-hand stuff for Cockshoot's; and if pigs could fly.... The Colonel shut the book with a bang and went out to the shed to look at the falcon. He smoothed the soft feathers. Khan was becoming much tamer.

He turned at the sound of footsteps behind him.

"I'm still after Cockshoot's," Moffat said. His bright little eyes blinked. The Colonel had never noticed before that one was blue and one was brown and that the brown eye squinted very slightly. The brown eye seemed to look at the hooded falcon. The blue one stared at the Colonel.

"It's not for sale," the Colonel said. It might be; he was already regretting the place, knowing they could never manage to get it done; could never sell this place; that all their plans were absurd and would come to nothing, but also determined that whoever bought it, it wouldn't be Moffat. Lisa would have to move if there was a huge pig farm beside her property. Moffat's pigs always stank; and he wouldn't change his ways. Nor would he make a good neighbour. The Colonel thought of the broken fences, the tangle of barbed wire, the pig sheds made of bits of corrugated iron, the pigs that wandered through the village street.

"You'll be sorry," Moffat said. "Shouldn't wonder if you have a job finding a buyer for this place. It's not everyone's cup of tea."

He grinned, showing broken brown teeth. The Colonel watched him walk away, his gross body wobbling. He smelled as bad as his pigs.

The man couldn't harm them; or could he? The Colonel found himself uneasy, wondering. Moffat was cunning. But where would he find the money for Cockshoot's? His own property wouldn't fetch a fifth of the buying price.

The Colonel climbed into the Land Rover, and drove to Deep Hollow, where Lisa gave him coffee and company and sympathy. She had baked a batch of scones, and they ate them hot, covered in fresh butter, which Lisa had taken to making from the milk of the Jersey cow that Tomkin had bought in a sale, at an absurd price because the animal was in bad shape, still being milked. Lisa had nursed the calf, and Lilac was now big and bonny and had given them two calves already, both of them sold at a good price to a neighbour with a pedigree herd, as Lisa had used his bull.

Paddy Joe was leading Thomas round the yard. The pony was livelier and up on his feet, but far from fit. Paddy Joe had fitted him with a key bit, making him take it when it was covered in toffee from the toffee apples. By the time he had sucked that off, he was resigned to the alien thing in his mouth. The Colonel thought he had never seen such a tiny pony. But the forlorn look in his eyes had vanished. He held his head proudly, and as Paddy Joe moved forward, Thomas butted him suddenly, and the Colonel could have sworn he saw a gleam of amusement in the brown eyes. Paddy Joe laughed and gave the small animal a tiny thump.

"You're getting too big for your boots," he said. "We'll have to stop spoiling you."

He shut the pony in the paddock, and vaulted the fence, crossing the field to Cockshoot's. Khan was on his fist. The bird was using his wings; stretching and trying them, longing to be away. He was very nearly healed. Paddy Joe was tempted to try him. He could not let him free, but he had in his pocket the long nylon line, the creance, that could be tied to the bird, to tether him, and let him beat against the air.

He fastened the line.

The bird watched him, curious, head on one side.

73

Paddy Joe rubbed Khan under the chin and he pushed against the scratching, the first response he had made.

Paddy Joe had made a lure, of chicken feathers, tied together. He tied a piece of meat to the lure, and lifted the bird. Khan flew, hanging on the air, pulling at the line.

He was stronger than Paddy Joe had imagined, and hard to hold.

He swung the feathers and the bird came at him, terrifyingly fast, landing with a solid thump, tearing at the meat. Paddy Joe lifted him and fed him more meat. It had worked. But the longing was there, to fly free and high. One day, but not yet.

Paddy Joe began to talk as he walked, softly, gently, soothingly and for the first time Khan bobbed his head in response, so that Paddy Joe felt eagerness overtaking him. He wanted to train his bird to the highest possible degree, to fly him free and have him return to the lure; he did not want to set him free. This was his bird. They were becoming a team, very slowly, very gradually, each day a little more response. There was a pride in owning him; a pride in holding him; a pride in watching him. And also the knowledge that this was no life for a wild bird, tamed and hooded and standing for hours on a block, alone, when he might be high in the sky, might be seeking a mate, might be breeding young of his own.

It was tempting to go on with him, to hide him where the Colonel and Tomkin would not find him, in one of the barns at Cockshoot's. There were so many of them, some divided into stalls; one had been obviously used for goats; another for calves; a third might almost have been part of a mews, where hawks were kept. The house was very old.

It was no use dreaming. There was work to do.

Later that day, helping remove the old staircase, he found a pair of shoes tucked into a recess by the top stair. They were rotting with age, the leather almost gone, the soles of wood, and two rusty buckles still in place.

"Good luck symbols, to bring fortune to the house," Tomkin said, when he saw them. "We'll bury them under the floor, Paddy Joe. Better not to court disaster by defying the old customs."

"Do you believe in those?" Paddy Joe asked, grinning.

"No, of course not," Tomkin said. "All the same, I always touch wood."

Paddy Joe laughed, but helped bury the shoes under the fireplace. The shape of the big dining room was now plain, the walls repaired, almost ceiling high. This had been one of the better parts of the house. Soon they would be up to the ceiling.

"They were an odd family," Tomkin said, perching himself on the trunk of a fallen tree in the dinner break. It was a fine day, the wind just touching the grass heads, and the sky blue and clear. Paddy Joe had brought the falcon with him. The hooded bird sat on his block under the tree. He was used to Paddy Joe now, who reached for the glove that lay by his satchel, put it on and lifted the bird to his fist.

75

"A lovely thing," Lisa said, looking at the speckled breast and brown wings. The bird heard her and turned his head.

"Tell us about Cockshoot's," Debbie said. "It's been empty ever since I came here."

"They were very rich once," Tomkin said. "Had a coachman and horses; a big stable, full of greys, all matched. The lads rode and hunted and the old man was a JP and something of a bigwig in these parts. That was before the last war. He was a small man with a big presence; you always knew when he came into the room. Grey haired when I knew him, nearing seventy, with a waxed moustache. A dandy in his clothes. There were five lads and three girls. The girls went to London for the Season and were presented at Court. They married and went away. The lads all went to war. Four of them died in France, and John Cockshoot came home blinded. The old man died soon after. The old lady had gone some years before. John Cockshoot never married. He lived there alone, with a man to look after him and slowly everything was sold off. He went away in 1962. No one has lived here since. It's been empty for sixteen years. Sometimes wonder if ghosts walk here. The house was built around 1500. The cellars are older than that. It's seen a lot of living."

Paddy Joe thought of the family that had lived here; and had vanished now, as if they had never been.

"Who did the house belong to?"

"John. And he vanished. No one knows where. They presumed him dead and then there was a long

76

legal wrangle as he had made no will and no one knew if he were dead or not and the three sisters were at odds over the place. The eldest claimed it as her right and the others wanted a part of it. They're still alive, I'm told, but they never meet or write to one another; haven't spoken for years. And the place just rotted."

It was time to get back to work.

Paddy Joe put his falcon back on the block and joined Chris, who was busy at the wood pile. It looked as if the day might change to rain and the wood needed covering. The tarpaulins were heavy.

"I've heard a rumour," Lisa said. "The vet was here today and says that Moffat is saying that the Government have their eye on the land all round your old home for opencast mining. Which will make it very difficult to sell."

"Opencast mining?" Paddy Joe stared, appalled. "Do you think it's true?"

Lisa shrugged.

"I don't know. But it's put two buyers off already, according to him. Have you had people cancel their appointments to view?"

Paddy Joe nodded.

The Colonel had stayed in twice in the last week for viewers, and both had phoned to say that they were unable to come.

"That's what the vet told me," Lisa said. "Be as well to tell Tomkin and get him to get your lawyers to look into it."

"But even if it isn't true," Paddy Joe said, "how

do we prevent people thinking it is? They'll say no smoke without fire."

"Moffat's got it in for us all, hasn't he?" Lisa asked.

"We bought this place," Paddy Joe said, looking at the house that was now beginning to take shape again. "And we bought the pony from him ... and you told him what you thought of him."

"And he's a bad enemy," Lisa said. "He's well known in the village for making trouble."

"He wants Cockshoot's. And if we don't sell my grandmother's house, then we will have to sell this," Paddy Joe said.

He felt as bleak as the clouds that came over the sun. All that money wasted. The interest on the loan; the fees for the various experts who had helped; the solicitors' fees.

Tomkin came over.

"What's to do, lad? You look as sick as a cat that's eaten a shrew."

Lisa told him what the vet had said.

Tomkin tightened his mouth.

"So he wants a fight," he said. "He'll get it. We're not going to be beaten that way."

"How can we fight when he will talk and spread lies?" Paddy Joe asked.

"There's more ways of killing a cat ..." Tomkin said. "The Colonel's a JP remember and he has several lawyer friends. We'll find a way."

Paddy Joe went back to work, clearing the ground inside the room next to the dining room. It seemed to have been used as a tip. Chris and Debbie were

78

working silently, filling sacks with rubbish flung there for decades. The clouds had massed and the sky was dark with rain.

Paddy Joe felt that the sun, would never shine again.

Chapter Six

A surprising amount had been done by the time the summer holidays were coming to an end. The site had been cleared, some of the walls re-built, and all the old timber removed and burned. Bonfires blazed daily. The caravan was installed in Lisa's yard, and the Colonel moved into it, so that he did not have to travel daily between his partner's home and his own. His main door was opposite the stable where Thomas spent his time. Paddy Joe had altered the high half door so that the pony could see out. His tiny head looked even smaller when Shadowfax leaned across him. The pony adored the big horse, and they spent much of their time together in the big field, nick-named the Long and the Short by Chris.

Casual passers-by, not looking closely, or perhaps not knowing horses, often mistook them for a mare and her foal, but Thomas was now growing into a chunky little colt, and some time they would have to cut him. The vet wanted to wait. He had a lot of time to make up for. The weals and scabs were healed, but his coat was not yet grown. And at times he had a cough, which came and went, but seemed not to disappear altogether. He had a passion for toffee, and Debbie often brought him home a few soft ones in her pocket, careful not to choose any that would stick his jaws together.

He was increasingly skittish, frisking in the field, kicking up his heels, coming to the gate to nibble at anyone who was wearing buttons, pushing his head against shoulders, or tucking his nose under an armpit, sure of his place among them, knowing they wanted him, and fussed him, and making the most of it. One day, Debbie was sure, he would be a show pony. When those bare patches vanished and his mane and tail gleamed silkily, and he had done some more growing. He had a presence about him, for all his tiny size. No one who enjoyed horses ever ignored Thomas.

Once Lisa had seen Moffat lurking near the stable yard. After that her big stud dog and two of the bitches always roamed free and the big gate was shut. None of the dogs ever jumped it, and people thought twice about coming inside unless their business was urgent or they knew the dogs.

When Lisa was not too busy, the pups that were being brought on for showing came outside too. They frisked around the Colonel's caravan doorstep and if he were not careful, came inside, where they created havoc.

The smallest of the pups was eight months old, an

extremely pretty little bitch that Lisa had bought from a family who had bred her, and who were reluctant to part with her, but who lived in a house that could not take three big German Shepherds. They already had her mother and her little sister.

She was a very gentle little bitch, full of importance, and under the impression that she was actually a retriever and not an Alsatian. She loved carrying things, and was often to be seen trotting round the yard with a huge piece of wood in her mouth, holding it proudly, head up, ears flat on her head, an expression of enormous pride on her face. Throw it for her and she was in heaven, running to bring it straight back so that it could be thrown again. Debbie was training her for the Obedience ring.

Since Lisa and the Colonel had become partners, Lisa had started boarding dogs again. Tomkin had made her a run of kennels, away from the house, with safety runs and passages between them so that even if a dog did get out, it was still not free to roam, but contained in another run bordered by chain link wire.

There were always dogs coming in and out. There were always people coming for dog food, or for puppies, or to bring a bitch to her stud dog. And sometimes Lisa had a rare day off, taking a bitch to a stud dog some distance away, leaving the rest of them in charge of the kennels.

She was taking one of the older bitches to a kennel in the North on the day Magina had her pups. Paddy Joe and Debbie were to be left in charge. Tomkin was taking the Land Rover to bring back a load of materials for building, and the Colonel was almost immovable with gout, sitting in the big armchair by the caravan window, with his bandaged foot on a stool, grumbling to anyone who had time to listen. He hated being inactive, but today he had no choice and the doctor had threatened him with hospitalisation if he did not obey orders. The Colonel could imagine nothing worse than being in a ward of old men, ordered about by a gang of pert young women. He did not consider himself old. Other people got old, even people the same age as he was, which struck him as most mysterious as when he was free from gout, he felt that he was still in the prime of life and as active as the next man.

The pups were free in the yard. Thomas was looking amiably over his stable door, and Magina, in her heated whelping box in the kitchen, was industriously cleaning up eight pups. She had had pups before and knew what it was all about. She nosed them contentedly.

"I've asked Tony to look in this afternoon," Lisa said, on her way to fetch her passenger from her kennel. Tony Haslett was the vet. "Shouldn't be any problems. I don't think there is another puppy there. She's in good shape and so are the pups. All you need to do is feed her. I've washed her down and put a clean blanket in the box. Be good, all of you."

There was work to do. As soon as she had gone Debbie began on the feeding of the dogs. With twenty of their own and eighteen boarders she was busy for the rest of the morning. Chris was already cleaning up, and putting dogs in the big compounds to run with each other and get exercise. Lisa had left a list of duties; of people who might call or phone; and of dogs, as some of them did not get on together and it was always necessary to watch the boarders. Some of them were only dogs, very spoiled, who attacked any other dog that came near, having been protected from other animals by fond owners. Some had odd feeding habits and two had special diets, one for a kidney disorder, and the other because he could not digest meat. They were separate and their food was separate.

There were the water bowls to re-fill. The pups to put in pens as the day was fine, a task that though pleasant, invariably took more time than Debbie allowed as they frisked and played with her and distracted her from work. All of them were penned on the island of grass beside the van, in front of the big picture window, so that the Colonel could keep an eye on them, and if anything went wrong, could ring the handbell that Lisa had begged from the village school when they installed an electric bell to signal the end of lessons.

Debbie was outside in the special kitchen that had been made from the old dairy. Here everything was kept, including the dog meal, the food in the deep freeze, the bowls and the measures.

Paddy Joe had the kitchen to clear up. They had all had breakfast together and as far as he could see, had used every dish and every pan in the place. He had Magina's bowl beside him, ready to fill with food for her. He put a big bowl of water down beside her, and was horrified to see her move suddenly and reveal two small hind legs protruding from under her tail. Another pup and the wrong way round and probably stuck.

He ran to the telephone.

Tony was out, and had been all night, at a farm twenty miles away, where a cow was in trouble, her calf also the wrong way round. There wasn't another vet anywhere near. The nurse suggested that Paddy Joe tried to ease the pup out, very gently, keeping both hind legs close together, to ensure he did not damage it.

Luckily Magina was a placid bitch. Paddy Joe remembered the drill and scrubbed his hands thoroughly. He bent over her, feeling the legs move in his hands. So the puppy was alive. Easy, easy, gently, gently, gently, holding his breath, afraid something would go wrong, something would happen that he didn't expect and suddenly and horribly afraid that this might only be half a puppy, without a head or legs, or deformed in some unusual manner.

And then it slipped into his hands, coming away so easily that he was again afraid of something wrong. He checked it carefully. It was quite normal. A small black bundle with a red nose, looking as unlike an Alsatian as any pup could. It looked more like a black rat. He dried it gently and handed it to Magina, who took it and finished the cleaning. It squeaked and yawned.

That was OK and then the afterbirth came away and he could clean her up and give her her food, and let her rest, the pups wriggling against her, nosing up to her, trying to feed from ear or nose or tail or to suck one another.

He looked at the clock. Two hours since he started the washing up. Time had flown and he couldn't believe that much time had gone....

He had just finished washing his hands again when the Colonel rang his bell, an angry jangle that sent Paddy Joe running outside. It was beginning to rain.

"Get those pups indoors," the Colonel said, when Paddy Joe put his head inside the van. Paddy Joe had guessed right.

Debbie was still making feeds for dozens of dogs. Lunch needed making but it would have to wait. There were three Alsatian pups in the first pen, now eight weeks, and waiting to be collected by new owners. They were adventurous and frisky and rounding them up was no joke. They were older, and could wait a little without hurt. The two West Highland Terriers were only six weeks old. Lisa was looking after them for a friend who was in hospital. They tucked easily under Paddy Joe's jacket and were soon indoors. He whistled in the dogs, who came racing, expecting food. He flung them bones as he shut the kennel door. By now the rain was beginning to fall in earnest and there were the other four Alsatian pups, now seven weeks old, needing to be carried in one by one.

Paddy Joe pushed two pups in with the Colonel. They were at least out of the wet. He ran, an Alsatian pup under each arm, to the second puppy kennel and put the two inside. The rain was teeming down and the two pups were wet. He dried them, and then, after some thought, took them into the kitchen, putting them in their pen near the Aga which was alight to keep Magina and her pups warm.

He looked at the clock.

Time for puppy feeding.

The Colonel's bell jangled again.

He had forgotten the other two pups. They had been running free, and there were puddles on the floor and the Colonel was angry. He was also hungry and impatient and not prepared to make allowances. Paddy Joe wanted to snarl back, but held his tongue knowing it would make matters worse. He took the pups and came back and cleaned the floor.

"I don't know how Mum copes," Debbie said, desperate, coming in for a large bucket, having mislaid the one she had started the morning with. "It's endless. When's lunch?"

"Heaven knows," Paddy Joe said. "I haven't fed the pups yet. Magina had one born after Lisa went; it was the wrong way round."

"Is it all right?"

"I hope so. It's moving as much as the others, and nothing seems wrong. Have to ask Tony when he comes."

"He'll be here before lunch if we don't get a move on," Debbie said. "I've still got eight dogs to see to. And I haven't started on the horses. And Thomas hasn't eaten his feed today. He looks droopy and miserable."

Always something, Paddy Joe thought savagely, making a start on mixing the powdered puppy milk which he added to the dog diet that Lisa used for rearing. Never seemed to have a moment free. And he hadn't had time to spare for his falcon. He was tame, but not yet tame, not yet trusting him, not yet his. And he never would be as the Colonel was insistent that as soon as the wing was mended, the bird was let free. He needed the sky, not the dark hut and the block to which he was tied.

Tomkin, driving into the yard with a spatter of gravel from the tyres, climbed out of the Land Rover, his face thunderous.

"Been busy all morning," Paddy Joe said.

"And so have I. I'll get lunch." Tomkin had seen the bitch in the box, noted the puppy plates and Paddy Joe's harassed expression and summed up right. "I went to Matthew this morning." Matthew was their solicitor, and an old friend of the family. "There is not any opencast mining scheduled, now or ever. There's no coal there. It was a total lie, put round to stop us selling. But Moffat's ahead of us. The story now is that there's subsidence, and we're selling quickly because the house has been condemned and will soon be pulled down. He was telling them that in the Black Swan last night and then went on to the Three Oaks, and told it again there. It's spreading like wildfire, that rumour, even quicker than the opencast mining story. And the devil of it is if we don't sell soon, we'll have to give up all idea of building Cockshoot's and sell that."

"Why is Moffat so anxious to have it?" Paddy Joe asked.

"That's what Matthew and I have been wondering. And we haven't come up with an answer.

He hasn't the money for a start; so he's either being sponsored by somebody else, or he's resources we know nothing about; and that doesn't seem likely, seeing the way they live. There's never been money to spare for anything over there."

"Except his beer," Debbie said acidly. She put the potatoes in the peeling drum, and turned the handle as if she would grind them all to nothing instead of peeling them.

"We don't want soup," Tomkin said, and she laughed, and took them out and put them in the pan, while Paddy Joe took out the puppy feeders, and supervised each group, and wished that he were free. Mostly, he found life fun, but today there were too many animals and too much to do and he was worried about the pup he had delivered. It would mean forty-five pounds less for Lisa and the Colonel if he had harmed it; and he'd never delivered a puppy before. Maybe he wasn't cut out to be a vet; even animals were a responsibility; each one had a life. Paddy Joe had once shot pheasants, but he found that now he could not kill, even for the pot, though he never minded eating those that Jake brought. We're all mixed up, he thought, as he closed the puppy kennel door.

The Colonel's bell rang again.

Paddy Joe sighed. The old man really was the limit today. He ran to the caravan.

"Damned animals," the Colonel said.

Suki, the Siamese Queen that Lisa kept for breeding had come into the van, and been sick in the middle of the carpet.

"Food," Chris yelled. Paddy Joe cleaned up. Suki helped him, by jumping on to his shoulder and rubbing against him, apologising, he hoped.

"She's been eating grass," the Colonel said, as the cat jumped to his knee and rubbed against him. She was one of his favourites and now the floor was clean he could forgive her.

Paddy Joe had eaten exactly two mouthfuls of his lunch when Tony drove into the yard. He was suddenly glad he was not yet grown up. Lisa did this every day; she sometimes complained she never had a moment to think, and he realised now that this was true. Not much time for eating either. He ran outside. Tony was looking over the stable door at Thomas.

"He's got a temperature," he said.

"He's off his food," Paddy Joe rubbed the pony's nose. "What do you think is wrong now?"

Tomkin had joined them, his face grim.

"Hear there's subsidence at your place," Tony said, as he examined the pony, running his hands expertly over its small body. Thomas rubbed his nose against the vet in an absentminded way, his mind on something that hurt, somewhere that none of them could identify.

"Then you hear wrong," Tomkin said. "Moffat's spreading that story, heaven knows why. I don't know what he is up to; he wants Cockshoot's; and goodness knows why he's so keen for just that place. There's others as good, if not better; I think all he wants is to spite us."

"Could be more to it than that," Tony said

thoughtfully. He filled a syringe. "I'll give him some antibiotic; but I honestly don't know what's wrong. He might be sickening for something. He hasn't much resistance, poor little devil."

"Moffat owes us a grudge for that," Tomkin said. "Maybe that's all there is to it. He's a nasty man to cross."

"You didn't report him. I would have done, for tuppence," Tony said. "I got him stopped from owning dogs; he was brutal to them. He owes me more of a grudge than you."

They made their way to the kitchen, where Magina greeted Tony, who she loved, and showed him the pups, proud of them as any human mother of her new baby. Tony praised and petted her and examined each one.

"Nice litter," he said approvingly. "Shouldn't be any trouble there."

"Is this one all right?" Paddy Joe asked anxiously. "It came hindlegs first and I had to help it out. I was afraid I might have hurt it."

"Looks fine," Tony said. He came to sit astride a chair and accept a cup of coffee. For a few minutes there was a break for all of them; a rest from doing.

But the time passed too fast, and Tony was off, back to take surgery, to cope with sick dogs and sick cats and inoculate puppies. And Paddy Joe had work to do; dogs to exercise and feed and clean out. He stopped beside Thomas to rub the pony's head, and pat him gently. But Thomas was lost in his own pain and took very little notice. Shadowfax, leaning over the stable partition, seemed to keep watch and offer reassurance. Life never went smoothly. Paddy Joe worked on.

Chapter Seven

Paddy Joe woke early. Morning was already bright, the sun promising heat. There was a haze over the garden. He could not stay in bed. He dressed, and took the dogs and went out into the sunshine. Gale and Storm raced round the overgrown lawn, sniffing at molehills, catching the scent of a rabbit that had passed over the ground, chasing the memory, abandoning it to come back and nose Paddy Joe, asking him to take them out on to the downs.

Paddy Joe was standing beneath the apple tree, lost to the present. Life was changing all the time, and he was suddenly and poignantly aware of it. This time next year he would not be able to stand here, remembering his grandmother. He had called her Grandee, which was short for Grande Dame, a name his father had given her long before he was born, teasing her. He couldn't remember his father or his mother. He had been only a year old when they died.

He remembered Grandee, stiff with rheumatism,

but determinedly tending her flowers, loving them, staking the delphiniums, growing a riot of colour in every bed. Tomkin had made over the flower bed to grass. It was easier to tend, with so little time for everything. Life had changed so much since Grandee had died. There had been a man every week to help her with the garden. Brian had loved his work. Together they had planned and schemed and planted. Some of their plantings were here still. The clematis that covered the south wall of the house with blue flowers every year; the rose that flung its rambling branches through the old plum tree that had borne fruit ever since he remembered.

There would be new people in the house, changing the rooms, making the place entirely different, living different lives here. And what would they do with the garden?

He had forgotten time and forgotten the dogs, lost in memory, surprised by his own reaction to change. He didn't want to leave the place. It was familiar, every inch of it, part of him and part of his life; all of his life, he thought with sudden insight. The house had helped to shape him. Here he had stood in the evening, while foxes played on the lawn and Tomkin had taught him to be still, to watch, to listen, to wait quietly. Here on this lawn Tomkin had shown him how to train his dog; how to shoot at the target on the post; how to cast a fly so delicately that it flitted over the grass, ready for the day when he would cast in the river and tease the tricky trout to snatch and hook itself. Here in this garden Tomkin had built him a barbecue and they

94

had cooked the fish they caught out of doors, and here too he had slept in his tent while Tomkin and the Colonel slept warm indoors.

There would be no memories for him at Cockshoot's. He saw the Colonel's viewpoint, and mirrored his fears. They would live in the caravan for ever, and they would never finish the building. Time would eat into their lives, and there would never be enough money. The horses would go, and then the dogs, and they would all be old. The Colonel was old; he would be gone and Tomkin too, and standing there in the bright sunlit garden, Paddy Joe felt panic overtake him at the thought of being alone in the world with no one of his own belonging to him; no one to talk to, no Tomkin to tease him out of a dark mood, no Colonel to shout at him because he had forgotten to clean his shoes or put out fresh water for the dogs.

The building had slowed down – school had begun. Time was running away with them and nothing was finished. And he was getting much too fond of Khan. He took the bird on his gloved hand. Khan bobbed his head and made a soft murmur of greeting. He could never let him free. The thought was unbearable.

The sun was behind the tallest tree and there were shadows on the lawn. The dogs were watching him. From the house came the smell of frying bacon. Lisa made the Colonel's meals. The house was somehow quieter without the old man. He was like Thomas, living inside his pain. Not relating to them, remote from them, seeing perhaps visions that had nothing to do with Paddy Joe or Tomkin; remembering times long gone when the world was younger and life moved at a slower pace.

"Wake up, lad," Tomkin's voice said in his ear. "No time for dreaming. Come and eat."

Paddy Joe walked into the kitchen. The lintel over the door was low, and he banged his head and stopped, startled, to look at the doorway which had become lower overnight.

"You've shot up in the night," Tomkin said, laughing at him. Paddy Joe had noticed before that Tomkin was shrinking fast. It had not occurred to him that it was he who was growing.

He rubbed his head. He would have to remember to duck, like the Colonel. Tomkin was smaller than the doorway. It was such an odd thought that it kept recurring, and he almost forgot to eat. Tomkin thought he was mooning over Debbie, but Paddy Joe was seeing things he had never seen before. The Colonel and Tomkin had always been bigger than him, and had helped him. Now he was stronger than either, and they needed him.

And Lisa needed his help too. She had far too much to do, all the time, and he had never realised it till yesterday. No wonder she was sometimes too tired to talk to them in the evening and sometimes snapped at Debbie, who used to help, but now was always out, determined to lead her own life and not be trapped by her mother's responsibilities.

Chris still helped. And Tomkin and the Colonel did what they could. But if they were going to build Cockshoot's, they needed more help than they

96

had. They couldn't neglect the dogs or the horses. If only there was someone he could talk to; someone who would understand his new worries that threatened at that moment to overwhelm him. If he had to stay around and help, he could never go to college; would never be a vet. And Tony had promised that next year he could help him in the long summer months, and learn practically.

His thoughts milled round in his head, uselessly, repeating themselves as he walked over the Deep Hollow, echoing madly as he looked at the shambles that was Cockshoot's, and finding more than echo when he went in to see how the Colonel felt.

The Colonel had woken to more pain and was fretful, complaining about nothing, sitting with his foot on a stool, exhausted by a sleepless night. Lisa had sent for the doctor.

"We'll have to sell to that fool Moffat," the Colonel said. "We can't do it, lad. Two old men and a boy and Lisa and Chris; Debbie's no help to anyone. Head over heels in love with that idiot."

Everyone was an idiot today but Paddy Joe heartily agreed with the term as applied to Debbie's latest boy friend. He was a first class prize idiot and Debbie was the only one that couldn't see it. All pretty manners and pretty phrases, based on some television hero, and didn't even know a horse's hock from its withers. Let alone know how to train or show a dog.

"Take my tray to Lisa and leave me to stew," the Colonel said, knowing he was not fit company for anyone. Suki was purring on his knee, unaware of his

97

mood. Suki was an odd cat. She tolerated people for a little while and then was liable to leap up and scratch them and run away. The Colonel preferred her to any of the more docile animals. He liked a bit of temper. In his day he had ridden only horses that behaved like rockets, full of fire and passion, needing mastery. Now he and his hunter were both old together, walking placidly, enjoying the mere act of being together as they had been so often in the past.

Lisa was making up puppy feeds.

"You did well yesterday," she said.

Paddy Joe found he had no answer. Praise was rare and made him uneasy, and he felt he had not deserved it. He took the pile of dog dishes and began to wash them up. Lisa raised her eyebrows, but said nothing.

Paddy Joe still needed to talk to someone. He shut the dogs in an empty kennel and cycled into the village. Tony was just leaving the house.

"I'm off to see a cow that has mastitis. Want to come?"

Paddy Joe needed no second invitation. The farm was nine miles away and there was time for talk. Time to tell Tony his fears; and to discuss Moffat's behaviour. If they didn't sell Grandee's home, they couldn't pay for Cockshoot's. And there were still no offers for the place. Tomkin had given the agent Lisa's phone number so that they could reach him there if need be and he would drive home to let viewers in. Only one man had called; and he had never been heard of again.

Tony listened without interrupting, his eyes on the road.

"I'll think about it," he said, as they drew into the farmyard. The farm was a big one, lapsing now into disrepair. Costs were too high everywhere. The huge old barns, covered in Russian vine in full bloom, were in need of new roofs and of fresh paint. The cobbles were weed covered. The house, red brick, weathered with age, slate roof covered in moss and lichen, lay warmly welcoming under the sun. The byres were spotless inside, though outside again they needed whitewash. Only the memory of that remained.

The sick cow was by herself. Tony examined her and injected her.

"Not too much wrong. You always get them in time," he commented. "No need to tell you to keep her milk apart from the rest until she is recovered."

"I'm an old hand," the farmer said, grinning. He was a small man, white haired and red faced, burned by wind and sun. He whistled to a small Jack Russell bitch who came running to jump at him, asking for affection. He rubbed her ears, and she ran from him to greet Tony and to sniff at Paddy Joe's legs, her tail wagging as she found the scent of other dogs, and knew at once that Paddy Joe was her sort of person. She leaned against him when he went indoors and sat on a stool by the hearth, while Tony and the farmer plunged into technical talk.

The farmer's wife was small, with dark hair and a

mischievous smile that lit up the whole of her face. She brought coffee and new baked scones, still hot from the oven, the butter melting over the sides, and a fresh baked cherry cake.

"It's a good job I don't have to come here often," Tony said. "You should ask for a piece of her new baked bread, Paddy Joe. That'll put muscle on you. You're growing so fast you're like an overstretched whippet."

"He'll fill out," the farmer said, his head on one side, making Paddy Joe feel like a cow being sent to market. "Only a whippersnapper as yet. Lots of growing sideways to do. He'll be a big man one day."

"Don't talk about him as if he wasn't here," his wife said, laughing at him. "You sum everyone up as if they were horses or pigs; it's a horrible habit."

"Summed you up all right, didn't I? Saw you standing there at the dance, looking as promising a piece of woman as I ever set eyes on."

"And that's enough of that. Have another piece of cake, Tony."

"Hear your grandma's place is up for sale," the farmer said, his mouth half full of scone. He had already eaten three and was into his fourth. His figure was beginning to show his indulgence.

"Yes," Paddy Joe said. He was cautious, learning all the time. Moffat's stories might not have reached this far.

"How much land is there?"

"Around thirty acres," Tony said. "Good grazing land."

The farmer fetched an ordnance survey map out of the cupboard.

"Where does it end?"

Paddy Joe pointed to the lane that formed the boundary. The farmer fetched a blue pencil, and made a line along the lane, and then a circle. The circle was on part of the Cockshoot's ground.

"That's where they hope to put the new golf course," he said. "They had their eye on Cockshoot's for the clubhouse, but there's another old place in better repair on the far side that would do as well."

"Is that generally known?" Tony asked.

"It is not. I'm on the planning committee and that's how I came to hear of it, but I think there have been rumours. Not only about a golf course, but about development there, which is not going to be allowed. A golf course wouldn't spoil the view and would add to the amenities. The nearest is over thirty miles from here. And it's up and down land, with plenty of hazards."

"So anyone buying Cockshoot's could ultimately make a profit from the land?" Tony glanced across at Paddy Joe.

"Too right, they could, in time. Not yet. But in the next year or so, that will come up and if the owners will sell, then they'll be adequately compensated. There's a big syndicate involved, interested in forming a company to make the course and run the place. It's stockbroker country, now that the farms are being sold off. That house of your grandmother's should fetch a good price."

"It's not fetching any price," Paddy Joe said.

"Someone's putting rumours around about subsidence, and other hazards," Tony said.

"And I can guess who. I was at the auction. Moffat's bidding for someone else, not himself. He hasn't that sort of money. I'll put the word around that the place is a good buy. It is a good buy, isn't it?"

"So far as we know," Paddy Joe said.

It was time to go.

"At least we know," Tony said.

"And what do we do? Moffat's told everyone; and people aren't going to buy something that's going to fall down on them. And they might not even bother to get the place surveyed. There's quite a few farmhouses up for sale round here. People are sick of being tied day and night, and they're getting out of farming."

"Don't I know it," Tony said. "Every time someone goes, I lose a bit more income. You want to specialise in small animals, Paddy Joe. Not farm beasts."

"But there aren't that many dogs in a village; and the towns are beginning to ban animals," Paddy Joe said.

"People are nuts. They'll turn the world into one big mental hospital. They kill off all life. We weren't meant to take over the earth and turn it into a concrete prison. Every time we make some creature extinct we remove a vital link in the chain of living. Everything belongs. Even rats can have their place in the country, by scavenging and I bet if they weren't scavenging in towns there would be a lot more filth than there is. Magpies keep the mice down. How many mice does your cat catch a day? Have you ever wondered?"

"Awful's always bringing in dead mice," Paddy Joe said. "He's only got to go outside for five minutes and he's found one."

"Think of them breeding uncontrolled by birds or beasts. They're immune to some of the poisons. Every time science finds out a new wonderful way of controlling something, it turns sour."

Tony was passionate, angered by the lack of knowledge among people who grew up away from reality, cocooned in cities where the sun only shone in the gaps between the great canyons of high buildings, where the only plants were sooty memories of the real thing, growing in tubs, where those that walked the streets were unaware of the sun on the far hills and the running deer; had never seen a fox come out of a brake, paw uplifted, scanning the horizon.

"People come to the country and see nothing," Tony said, pursuing his own train of thought and incidentally driving faster, as anger took him. "They come in hordes to see rare plants and trample the plants out of existence. They come in swarms to see ospreys breed and the birds can be put off and refuse to feed their chicks."

"We went to Wales last year," Paddy Joe said. "There's a beach on Anglesey, protected by wardens. They've staked out the beach with numbered posts, and when I was walking the dogs there, a man in a Land Rover asked me to keep away from the area between posts 17 and 23, as the ring plover were nesting. We walked at the sea edge, and watched them, looking for food on the stones and under the seaweed for the chicks."

"Khan's nearly tame," he went on. The bird was always in his thoughts. It was becoming a passion so that he spent less time with the dogs and the horses. Tomkin did not approve. Dogs needed training. Horses needed exercise. "I don't want to let him go."

"He was born free," Tony said. He braked and stopped the engine. They were high on the downs with sheep running below them, moved by a man with a collie dog. A lark soared above them, and beyond it the sky was clear blue, wide and peaceful.

"Would you want to be earthbound all the time, with that as your heritage?" Tony asked.

Paddy Joe shook his head.

He looked out, using his eyes as Tomkin had taught him to do. There was a movement across the fields, and a hare bounded slowly, and then sat, washing itself, catlike, using its paws to squeeze each ear as if it were draining water from the fur. He hardly saw it. He could only think of Khan.

Somewhere a stick snapped, cracking gunlike in the silence and the hare was away, leaping towards the hedge, and vanishing as if it had never been. With the crack came a flurry of wings as pigeons rose from feeding on a fallow field, and a covey of partridges followed them. The country that had been so still, apparently devoid of life, was suddenly noisy with bird calls, alarm sounding on alarm.

"Lift a stick at feeding crows or pigeons and watch them fly," Tony said. "And take a falcon in a van to a place where you have hunted before and you won't see a single bird. They know the van and remember the falcon, and stay close hid. They learn, fast."

He put the engine into gear.

"Tomkin's tired and the Colonel's old, Paddy Joe. You're going to have to take some of the responsibility for them. It's time. You're almost seventeen. They looked after you; now it's your turn."

"I know," Paddy Joe said. "And there's Lisa too. Debbie isn't much help."

"You can't take them all on, for heaven's sake. Come and lunch with us. And let's see if we can think of a way to get Cockshoot's moving; and to outwit Moffat. The Colonel will drive himself mad with worry if something doesn't happen soon. He's withdrawn into himself and no one is getting through. It would be a pity to have him give up; it's a good partnership. And Lisa is beginning to make a profit. She breeds splendid pups; and she knows what she's doing. We can't lose her knowhow. She can teach you a lot, Paddy Joe. Only you have to listen. No use thinking you know it all. You never stop learning. If you do stop learning, you might as well be dead."

Lunch was ready. A shepherd's pie, flavoured with unusual herbs, that stretched with extra cabbage and potato to feed all of them; an apple pie with cream from Tony's Jersey cow, a recent acquisition that Paddy Joe was taken to admire. Toffee was caramel coloured with wise brown eyes, dark fringed with long lashes. The sorrowful circles round them belied her nature as she was frisky and butted Tony playfully before nudging into his pocket to look for the goodies he always carried there.

It was time to return, but Paddy Joe felt as if he had had a holiday. Freedom from worry and rides in a car. It was half of a well remembered quote and he said it aloud.

"The dormouse and the doctor," Tony said promptly, closing the paddock gate on Toffee, who had every intention of following him to the kitchen door.

Paddy Joe had a memory of being a small boy, seated by the fire, while Martha, Grandee's house-keeper, read to him.

"The dormouse lay there with his paws to his eyes,
And imagined himself such a pleasant surprise ...
Martha used to read it, but that's all I can remember; not even what it was about."

"The dormouse liked delphiniums blue and geraniums red," Tony said. "The doctor ordered different flowers planted, so that when he was surrounded by all the wrong kinds of flowers for him, he lay there with his paws over his eyes, imagining that nothing had changed. Like most of us, he was afraid of change."

Paddy Joe thought of Tony's words as he cycled back to Deep Hollow. Changes came, all the time. You knew in advance they were coming yet somehow when they did come, they were sudden. You knew for years you would leave school at eighteen; be grown up and out in the world. Perhaps go to college. But even though you wanted it to happen and waited for it to happen with impatience, when it came, it was as sudden as if you had never anticipated the coming and perhaps the reality was never as you imagined.

He remembered his first show with Storm. Both of them had known the exercises and Storm, at home, worked perfectly. Paddy Joe had known he could go into the ring and win. And yet, when it came to the point, the ring was not like the quiet garden where they trained. There were other dogs running around, people playing ball with their dogs, a bitch that ran into the ring and out again, distracting Storm, and they ended up nowhere. It had taken months of showing to settle him, to learn to ignore distractions, to concentrate all the time and even then things went wrong.

And then there had been the totally unexpected day when everything went right and they did win, just when he had given up all hope of ever showing how well he and his dog could work together.

Now, he was soon to leave school; and he had no idea whether he would achieve his ambition to be a vet, like Tony, or would have to make do with some other job. They were leaving the home that had been his for years; and embarking on something that looked quite crazy. He thought of Cockshoot's, needing far more work on it, needing weeks of work, needing materials which it absorbed into itself like some greedy dragon eating money. And their own home still waiting for a buyer.

He paused to look down on Deep Hollow, cuddled into the ground, the trees behind it swaying in the wind that threatened soon to be a rip-roaring gale. There were dogs, dwarfed by distance to the size of mice, racing in the yard. Chris must have let them out for their daily exercise, to race against one another in the paddock, tails streaming behind them, legs covering the ground, in a flying pack of Alsatians, running with the wind, while the foals came to canter alongside, and the mares stood watching benignly, born on the farm, the dogs a part of their daily lives. The dogs never chased them, though sometimes the young pups ran at them, and were then checked by a huff, a snort and a stamp from the giants they were so bravely defying.

Perhaps later there would be time to ride Shadowfax, out on the downs, if his leg was better. He was still slightly lame, and Paddy Joe had had to walk him, and not ride him, but exercise the horse on his halter, striding out beside him, for the past few weeks.

He mounted his cycle and free-wheeled down the hill, the wind in his hair, the hedge flying past him, a breathless elation seizing him, as he sped on. Then it was uphill, and into the yard, where the dogs were just returning from their run, tongues lolling, panting. They ran to the trough to drink.

Paddy Joe leaned his cycle against the wall and went to talk to Thomas. But Thomas was standing lacklustre, not responding even to a voice. His coat was dull and staring, his eyes mattering and above him Shadowfax, leaning over the partition, seemed to brood anxiously.

Lisa came across the yard.

"I've been trying to get Tony all afternoon," she said. "Thomas wasn't too bad this morning, but look at him now. It's not a germ; Tony was positive of that yesterday. But something is very wrong."

"Never rains but it pours," Tomkin said. "Gale's cut her pad half off on glass. She won't be showing on Saturday, Paddy Joe. And she'd a chance there. No point in just taking Storm. You can help with Cockshoot's."

Paddy Joe remembered what he had heard about the golf course, but Tomkin had gone, to try and stop Gale's pad bleeding, and Lisa was not in a mood to listen.

"The Colonel's asleep. The doctor came and gave him an injection to ease the pain and he's making up for lost nights," Lisa said. "Don't disturb him."

"I'm off," Chris called, as he ran by, dressed in his Scout uniform.

"Debbie's out too," Lisa said. "Can you see to supper, Paddy Joe? It's all ready; salad and tongue and cold potato salad and there's a fruit pie. I must do something for Thomas, though heaven knows what."

She vanished inside the stable.

Paddy Joe went indoors thinking irritably how absurd it was to be surrounded by people and yet never have anyone there who had time to talk.

He jumped as something landed on his shoulder.

It was Awful, wanting food.

Paddy Joe fed him, and laid the table, evicting two of the cats who were anxious to steal the cream. Tomkin appeared from the stall opposite, leading Shadowfax. The horse was still limping. The injury refused to heal. If only he hadn't jumped that hedge....

If ifs and ans were pots and pans there'd be no work for tinkers.

Martha always said that.

The wind was growing, raging through the trees and the sky was midnight dark. Lightning lanced across it and Tomkin hurried the horse inside, as rain poured from the angry clouds, lashing on the corrugated iron roofs, drumming on the cobbled yard. Paddy Joe ducked his head and raced to put the dogs indoors, to rescue three pups from the puppy pen and take them in and dry them and switch on the heated bed for them, to avoid chilling.

When he returned the cats had jumped in through the window and eaten the tongue. He fetched a tin from the pantry, and opened it, cursing, only to cut himself on the jagged edge.

He stood, blood pouring from his finger, washing it under the tap.

"Never rains but it pours," Tomkin said, reaching for a towel to dry his hair.

Paddy Joe glared at him, feeling like hitting him. Everybody was too stupid for words, and nothing ever went right. Not ever.

He swathed his hand in a bandage, and Lisa, coming in soaked, at once pulled it off, put antiseptic on the cut and bound it neatly with plaster.

"You're hopeless, Paddy Joe," she said.

He had been going to tell them about the golf course but now he wouldn't. They could stew and worry all they liked and leave him in peace. The thunder crashing above him reflected his mood. He wanted to shout at them, to throw things. But instead he sat quietly, and ate, tasting nothing.

If this was being grown up they could keep it. He wished he was a small boy, able to run and hide, to sit in the apple tree while the grown-ups talked of things he knew nothing about. Once he had thought being grown up was an end to all problems.

Now he had a horrible feeling that it was only the beginning of more than he had ever dreamed could exist.

The rain was easing.

Lightning flashed again and then there was a glow in the sky, and Paddy Joe, turning his head, saw a flaming ball hover over a tree, heard a crack like the sound of doom, and the tree split down the middle, neatly, like a peeled banana, and fell in slow motion, half to one side, half to another.

Outside in the yard dogs were howling, Shadowfax was kicking in his stall and one of the mares was squealing, her voice high and frightened, startling off the other horses.

Everybody ran.

In the empty kitchen the cats climbed back on the table and finished the meat at their leisure.

Chapter Eight

The little man appeared like a genie at the kitchen door while Lisa was washing puppy dishes. He grinned at her, and took off his cap.

"Farmer that Tony saw yesterday tells me you're building," he said.

"Yes." Lisa looked at him doubtfully. Paddy Joe, who had been cutting up dog meat, for the older dogs who were still fed in the old fashioned way, unlike the pups, fed on a dry all purpose diet, stopped work.

"We're doing it ourselves," he said. The Colonel had been grumbling about the amount of money even that took. And there still was no buyer for their house.

"That's all right, lad." The old man came into the kitchen. Lisa put the kettle on. No one ever came to see her without being given coffee and cakes. "I was a master builder, used to work with old Josh. He sent me over. He's far from well. I retired four years ago. And all day long I sit and get in my old woman's way, or go down to the library and read the paper where it's warm. Nothing to do; nowhere to go; nothing to plan for. Nothing to achieve. That's not living, lad. It's hell. Waiting till they put me in a box. There's half my old gang in the same boat. Len and Jack and Bob, as well as me. I can turn my hand to anything. Len's a plasterer. Jack's a brickie and Bob's the man that did the roofs. We'll come and do it for fun; don't want paying. Just want to be useful. I know we're all retired, but we aren't past it, not any of us. None of us lives in the sort of place that gives us a chance to build. Done that long ago. And we've all got wives that would jump for joy if we got out of their roads."

"You're on," Tomkin said. He had come in and stood quietly, listening. "You'll be a godsend. We can't get to it every day. And though we've had some help, its comeday, goday, and they get tired and stop coming."

"Come and show us the site, lad, if you're free after coffee," the old man said. He was neatly dressed, his grey suit well pressed, his tie surprisingly gay and flowery. Bright blue eyes lightened his dark face.

It was fascinating to listen to the old man talking. His name was Sid Evans. He had been apprenticed to a builder when he was fourteen years old, learning the trade, starting with digging foundations, learning to plaster, learning to work with wood.

"No unions in those days to say this man could only do one part of a job and that one another," he said. "We'd swop over. Less boring. I can turn my hand to anything now, from tiling to bricklaying; and do as good a job as the next man. I'm a fair decorator too."

He looked the site over with practised eyes, walking into every corner, bringing out a measure to size up a room, noting down figures in his little exercise book and making calculations that Paddy Joe couldn't even begin to understand.

"Have to watch the drains outside," he said, eyeing the land. "Field slopes up, away from the house and will drain down; could get the place flooded if we don't put the drains in the right place. And it could make it damp. There's a fair old job there, lad."

"We won't do it," Paddy Joe said miserably, thinking they had been insane. "And no one wants our house either."

"I know someone who might," Sid said. He was a puckish little man with a lined face that was all seams and hollows, but his eyes were brilliantly alive and often alight with laughter. "Friend of mine. He's turning his farm over to his son and looking for a place with a bit of land, with outhouses where he can stable a couple of horses; with an orchard for the goats. He breeds Golden Guernseys. Pretty things. You don't often see them here. Tomkin was telling me there's a big old building that used to be a cow byre before your grandmother's day, still in good repair."

"Do you want to see it?" Paddy Joe asked.

"All in good time, lad. There's a lot to look at here,

and to work out. I can get at least four of my friends;
maybe five. Think of it, lad, out every day on the
job again, making something to last; and we've
time, all the time in the world, all the rest of our
lives. Time to do it well, time to look for good
second-hand materials; time to build a brick fireplace,
and add all those touches we never could before
because of the need to keep within a tight budget.
Even now, we can get you doors for the inside
rooms, doors such as you won't buy these days,
for practically nothing, from a dealer who buys in
from condemned houses, or from old stately homes,
being pulled down; wonderful stuff going begging.
People don't know what they're missing, getting this
rubbish from the wood yards, unseasoned stuff, likely
to split. No one builds the way they did in my young
days."

Paddy Joe left him happily probing and poking
around Cockshoot's and went back to Thomas, who
had been given an injection, but he was not
feeding and he looked at Paddy Joe from lacklustre
eyes.

There was little he could do for the pony, but he
fetched the grooming tools and began to brush him
gently, hoping that the presence of someone doing
something for him would help. Thomas moved his
head, butting gently against Paddy Joe, and then
leaned against him.

Sid, coming into the stable unannounced, made
Paddy Joe jump.

"What's up with him, then?" he asked.

"Goodness knows," Paddy Joe said, shrugging.

"Even the vet couldn't find anything wrong when he examined him."

"I had a pony go like that once. It's a long time ago now. Little Shetland, very like this fellow. Let's be at you, little lad." Sid was beside the pony, his hands exploring gently. "My Dad bred Shire horses. I'd have liked to but by then we'd no money and had to sell. Motors destroyed the horse industry. Nasty smelly things. I'd sooner have a horse any day. Ah, here it is. Feel this lad, down under his belly, in the angle of the leg."

Thomas flinched as Paddy Joe put his hand against the soft hide. There was the smallest indication of a swelling, just under the skin.

"It's a deep abscess. Been coming for a week or so. Be some time before it comes to a head, and it's only just swelling under the skin now. That's why the vet never spotted it. Need fomentations, lad, and we'll get it to a head and burst it. He'll be right as rain when that happens. Take a bit to get over it, mind."

There was always something with a horse. Sweet itch, from insect allergy, capped elbows through bruising itself on one leg with the shoe on another leg; laminitis in the foot, horses unfit for all kinds of reasons from not enough exercise to foaling. When Sid returned with the antiphlogistine that Lisa kept for poultices, Paddy Joe voiced his thoughts.

"You know a bit," Sid said.

"I want to be a vet."

"Interesting job." Sid was busy, soothing the pony,

hissing to him, handling him carefully, while Thomas stood quiet, trusting this newcomer who had huffed into his nostrils and spoken softly. Paddy Joe went on combing the long mane. Soon he would have to return home, to help Tomkin, and feed his hawk. Khan now flew regularly on the creance. Paddy Joe wanted to fly him free. But suppose he refused to return? He didn't want to lose him yet.

Thomas was tugging tentatively at his haynet. He turned and put his head against Paddy Joe's arm, tucking underneath it. They stood companionably, looking out at the stable yard where Awful was busy stalking a wisp of hay that blew in front of him. He pounced and missed and yawned, and then sat, indignant, licking at a frantic paw, as if his life depended on it. Paddy Joe knew better than to laugh. Awful hated being laughed at.

Gale nosed him, but he was thinking of other things; wondering about the abscess and how soon it would burst; wondering about Sid, who seemed to know a great deal about a great many things. Gale butted him, and began to dance in front of him, impatient.

"Have you fed Gale?" Lisa called.

Thomas dug an impatient nose into Paddy Joe's pockets. There were two dog biscuits there, put in as titbits for later, when he and Storm started working together. Storm was getting bored and over trained and tonight was to be a play night with food as a reward, just to make a change. But the biscuits had gone; Thomas was beginning to take notice again, although he was far from well. Paddy Joe rubbed the soft velvety nose, and closed the door behind him.

Thomas returned to his haynet, and Shadowfax started on his, apparently feeling his days as nurse-maid were over.

Sid came back into the yard. He had an air of importance about him that had been lacking before, and a notebook now full of figures. He walked over to the stable.

"He'll do," he said. "Time I looked my sheep over. Like to come, lad? I've a little flock of my own down the road. I inherited some lambs from my brother, and kept the best of them." He chuckled suddenly. "Reminds me of a poem we learned at school. 'Nine bean rows will I have there, and a hive for the honey bee.' Well, there's no beans there but nine fine ewes have I got there, and my hive is two hives; I'll bring some honey tomorrow. Feed your dogs, lad, and then I'll be showing you."

It never took long to feed the dogs; a pound of dog diet and hot water to release the smell; it was finished almost before it was down and the dogs had a brief walk and then were put to rest in the end stall beyond Shadowfax. No running immediately after a meal. That could cause bad trouble.

Paddy Joe followed Sid down the lane. Clouds were masking the sun; the evening light was changing, the glow beyond the horizon deepening to red. There was a stillness in the air; the wind of the early day had died and the world was waiting. There was a brooding excitement, a feeling that time was standing still, tomorrow would be a new beginning, a gateway to a future beyond belief.

It was an odd sensation; Paddy Joe thought it had something to do with Sid, who was walking as if he had been given the most wonderful present in the world, his pork-pie hat pushed jauntily back on his head, and he was whistling.

The lane ended and they turned on to the main road; not a big road, but wider than the lane, allowing cars to pass between the hedges. There was no path. The hedges were overgrown; tangled masses protruded into the road. Soon they would trim them with the big machines that wrecked them for a season, leaving torn bare twigs that were an outrage, pointing bleakly at the sky, until the new growth hid and softened them, and the ruin was forgotten in the wild overgrowth of midsummer.

The little field was triangular; the grass cropped short, and the ewes were grazing. Sid's face lightened as he saw them and he leaned over the gate, holding a paper bag in his hand, whistling and calling.

"Coom, my pretties, coom, coom; coom and see what I've got for you."

The eager black heads went up, the ewes marched towards him and then, as he held out the bag, the march became a stampede and they reached the gate, baaing and pushing and jostling, trying to be first to receive the bread crusts from his fingers. He slipped through the kissing gate, and as each one came to him, ran his hands expertly over its body, and patted it on the nose.

He grinned at Paddy Joe.

"A man needs a family," he said. "Mine are all

grown up; busy with their own lives, and my old woman's busy with the house; prinks it and polishes it till it's like sitting in a glasshouse; don't dare to smoke, or put a dirty shoe inside her polished hall, or bring a pal in. And in the evening she looks at the gawk box, the people in it more real than I am. Coronation Street; you'd think they lived next door, that lot, more important than our Bess having her baby, or my ewes lambing."

Paddy Joe thought of the people around him, always busy with their own affairs, sometimes pausing a little to speak to him, yet not really listening. Tomkin forever with one eye on the Colonel, the Colonel immersed in his own pain, Lisa always thinking of the dogs; Debbie of her new boy friend and only heaven knew what went on in Chris's head. He knew exactly how Sid felt, wanting to talk and no one to listen.

"How long have you been retired?" he asked.

"Four years; seems like all my life. Suddenly everything ends; pointless, every day the same. No looking forward to Saturday; it's just like Monday or Tuesday. Nothing to get up for; nowhere to go. No one waiting for you. You hold your hand out for your pension like a little boy asking Daddy for his pocket money. Been a good boy all me life and now having me reward, only it don't go nowhere much. That's why I keep the sheep; money for wool and money for lambs. It helps. And it's an interest. In winter, I got to come out and give them hay or they starve; this field isn't big enough, but it's all I have."

"There's lots of room at Cockshoot's," Paddy Joe said, his mind suddenly taking a great leap into the future, seeing the fields full of grazing sheep and in the spring the lambs frisking and playing, bringing in money for them. Sid could be shepherd.

Sid might have been telepathic; he had had the same thought.

"I like sheep," he said. "Born on a farm, but there wasn't the money to keep it going, so I got into the building trade; or rather, me dad put me there. Pays your money and takes your choice, they say, but for lots of people there never is no choice. Take any job so long as it feeds the wife and the kids. Go on doing it all your life, one day after another, doing the best you can; from five years old to sixty, Monday to Friday, working every day; and then it stops. Unless you find a new goal, a new way to live, you might as well give up. There's nothing to go on for. Without me sheep ..." Sid contemplated a world without sheep and found it completely horrible.

"They've all got names," he said. "There's Rosie and Posy; and Carrie and Sally; and Jilly and Milly; and that one's Contrary Mary. She's the boss, the mischief maker, and she can get into mischief too. She breaks through the hedge and trots out; or kicks all the lambs away from her own lamb and then there's trouble, you never heard such a din as when that starts. I lost me dog this year; old Ben, he'd herded for me for all the time I had the sheep though he wasn't trained to it. He was a pet first, but he never came indoors and Poll won't let me have another. Makes too much work, feeding the dog and as to a pup . . . well, you'd think I'd suggested bringing a calf indoors."

"You could keep a dog at our place," Paddy Joe said.

"Finish that and I've a feeling we could all have a new start in life," Sid said. "There'll be plenty to do, just keeping the place going; and if we can help, and maybe have a bit of ground where we could grow our own food by way of payment. . . ."

The sun was dying in the sky, the night reaching out towards the trees. There was a faint star high above them and the ghost of a small moon, a shadow of its former beauty. Paddy Joe looked up and the sky darkened and the stars leaped into life and the moon glowed into a thin crescent, a shining slender horn, a star gleaming beside it. There were worlds beyond him. Remote, distant, dwarfing man, making his affairs insignificant. This sky had looked on Roman boys, exiled in a chilly land far from home, on British boys, resenting the conquerors; on boys in Elizabethan times, fearing the rack because they boasted the wrong religion; they would look down on another boy in a distant future when no one remembered him, or Sid, or the troubles that bedevilled them. On a better world? Who knew. Maybe the Dark Ages would come again and the spirit of man would have to fight the forces of Evil all over again; and would that spirit triumph?

"Never give in, lad," Sid said. "Never give up. And never let anyone talk you into doing something against your conscience. That's what my dad used to say. It's stood me a long time in good stead. You're my kind of lad; I wish my sons had been, but they wanted the bright lights and the cities; no time to stand and stare."

He stopped. There was white heather growing in the bank. He picked a spray. "For luck for all of us," he said. "We'll plant it at Cockshoot's. A great bank of it, right where you can see it in the morning from the dining-room windows. We'll build a house to be proud of, a house for the future; a house for your grandchildren to remember. In fifty years' time the sun will still set on it, standing as firm as ever."

He looked up at the sky and grinned.

"Poll'll think I've bin drinking again," he said. "Time I was off. Come to think of it I feel flown tonight but not with beer; with something to do again; to be part of the world again, making my mark again. Sid Evans, his mark. Maybe that's why kids write on lavatory walls; to leave something for someone else, and they don't know no better than to write rubbish. We're going to write poems for posterity, lad." He laughed at Paddy Joe's expression. "I like long words though I sometimes get 'em wrong. Had to teach myself. I left school at fourteen; kids today, they have a better chance but they don't want it. We had no chance and we did want it. Contrary, aren't we?"

He turned away and plodded up the road, but to Paddy Joe he walked as if he was seeing visions; a little old man forgotten by the world, brought back to life by the promise of a future that he had never thought existed until today.

Another responsibility for Paddy Joe, he thought, seeing how his life might be changed, might be dominated by the needs of others rather than his own, and yet, if they could all work together, could make it work, he would be free to go off and study, and come back to set up here, perhaps with Tony, qualified as a vet himself.

The stars looking down were a symbol of eternity; of time speeding by, watching over so many lives, world without end, for ever.

A promise; a growing excitement, a feeling that a future waited, that he only had to reach out and it would fall into his hands; that here in the night was the answer to all the mysteries, to all man's wonderings, to all man's fears. Here was the gateway to adulthood.

An owl flew by on softly whispering wings.

Far away the church clock chimed the hour. Time had started again and would not wait for him or anyone.

Whistling, Paddy Joe leaped the gate and ran all the way home.

Chapter Nine

Paddy Joe had never met anyone like Sid. He was an enthusiast, loving everything he did, even if it was only laying one brick on another, aligning it perfectly, stepping back to see that it was straight. He kept up a constant flow of talk as he worked, cheering the others on, making small jokes that were rarely very funny, but that raised smiles and roused the men with him to double their efforts.

Paddy Joe realised that for all of them this was a new beginning, was something to do after years of inactivity. Four years of doing nothing with nowhere to go had sapped them, but this was a return to youth and strength came with it, as unaccustomed muscles were brought into action.

By the end of ten weeks, the men who worked with Sid were looking alive and alert again, had shed years in age, were singing as they turned the rubble back into a house. Paddy Joe was living two lives; by day at school, and then a race back to Cockshoot's to see what progress had been made, to share his tea with Sid, who talked as he ate, using knife and fork to illustrate a point.

"The bath here; the basin there. Separate WC. A shower in the downstairs cloakroom; we can all turn our hand to woodwork, build you cupboards, put up shelves." It was a plea and a statement all in one.

Sid glanced at the Colonel.

Progress was helping him too. He could see the shape of the house at last; walk through the reconstructed rooms, help clear the rubble from the inside, stand in the kitchen, watching it develop to the stage where plans became possible again. Sid's friend was buying their house; in time the money for that would come through and they were getting a good price. Life in the caravan was smooth; there was little to do but tuck the sleeping bags away during the day and clean the floors. They all ate with Lisa, who in her turn enjoyed the company of adults. Debbie and Chris were diluted to a point that no longer mattered. Chris, not needing to help so much, was less of a trial, and his clumsiness was reduced to almost nothing as people stopped grumbling at him.

"Chris is all top dressing and underneath he's afraid," Sid said, on one particularly disastrous occasion, when Chris had tripped over a dog bowl he had forgotten to pick up from the yard and smashed three dozen eggs. The resulting mess had to be seen to be believed, but the dogs and the cats had a field day. Chris, told off for his carelessness, had forgotten to shut the door of the puppy kitchen, and the older dogs had cleared up three days' food, and slept off the result, worrying everyone because they slept so long.

Grumbling at Chris made him worse. This time Lisa was furious, as food cost money and the older dogs had had far too much, and would suffer. Chris, told not to slam the kitchen door, left it wide open.

This time the cats came in and the meat for supper, waiting on the draining board when Lisa was called to the phone, vanished in its turn.

"Damn cats, damn dogs, damn boys!" Lisa yelled.

"They're only young once," Sid said, coming in to the kitchen on hearing her shout. He had come across for tea. He took over from Lisa.

"Go and sit down, love. I'll do the makings."

Lisa looked at him.

"I don't know what you'll do the makings of," she said. "The cats have cleared the decks; and Chris has taken care of most of the eggs and I just can't think any more."

"Can I hunt the pantry? I used to be a dab hand in the army; Poll never lets me near the kitchen." His voice was wistful.

Old men were just like little boys, Lisa thought, recognising the note that came into Chris's voice when he wanted something badly.

Sid made a pot of tea and brought Lisa a cup. It was good to be waited on, good to sit down for once and not think, to hear Paddy Joe and Tomkin busy in the yard. Thomas's abscess had burst the

evening before and Thomas was already a different
pony; full of himself and wicked with it, butting them
when they came near him in what was apparently a
passion of love. Thomas adored everyone and wanted
to be adored; he wanted it so badly he tried to
climb under their coats, putting his head and one
fore hoof hard into those who came near him. He
and Shadowfax were inseparable, calling to one
another whenever one was removed from the
stable, making the place noisier than the dogs.
Shadowfax had a powerful squeal. And Thomas had a
voice belonging to a much bigger animal and liked to
use it, blaring to Debbie when she came home from
school, yelling to Paddy Joe as he rode into the yard,
screaming to Chris to come here quick and bring
toffee apples, rewarding Sid with a nibble and a swift
detaching of another button from his coat which Lisa
hurriedly sewed on again, as Poll would grumble.
No one had ever seen Poll; she became a sort of
ogress when Sid had gone, keeping the old man in
order, neat and tidy, imprisoned in the narrowness
of her own life.

At Deep Hollow and Cockshoot's, Sid shed his
home personality and became a totally different
man, driving everyone with his enthusiasm, talking
eagerly to the Colonel about sheep. All kinds of
sheep.

Later that evening Paddy Joe went to see how the
work was progressing. The electricity was connected,
the roof was finished, the rooms were re-plastered,
the floors were half laid, the windows were glazed. It
was a house with a future now, not a derelict ruin. No

one wanted to go home. They all wanted to finish, to see it lived in and furnished, and each one planned what he would put in each room, given the chance. The place was noisy with hammers and saws, with an electric drill used on the upper floor, with the swishing of a plane, as the woodwork master from school had come back to help with the carpentry, having a passion for all kinds of wood.

"Smooth as silk," was his favourite phrase and he spoke sometimes to Paddy Joe of his own dream, never realised, because he had no money to back himself, of making furniture that would rival Mousy Thompson's. He showed Paddy Joe his treasure, a pair of Mousy Thompson bookends, the wood adzed instead of being planed, the grain shining; and on each was carved a little long tailed mouse that was the trademark of the firm. The old man was long dead, but his work went on and craftmade wooden articles came from the workshops; some for the tourist market, some for export, some being used in churches still, where a Mousy Thompson lectern was an heirloom.

"There's a little church in Yorkshire, Hubber-holme, I think the place is called ... so long since I been there," Sid was remembering. "Every pew has a little mouse on it somewhere, perhaps down the side, or under the seat or at the base of the end piece. And it's there on the lectern too. Spent a whole day there once when my lads were small, shel-tering from a thunderstorm, picking out the little mice," Sid said. "Lovely work." He rubbed a finger along the gleaming polished wood, sharing the woodwork master's reverence for a splendid piece of craftsmanship.

He left soon after and Paddy Joe worked for a while with the men, fetching and carrying, absorbed in watching them, fascinated by the way each moved, long years in the job having taught them the quickest and easiest way to handle saw or plane or chisel. Their pride in their work increased daily, so that each now paid a fanatical attention to detail, trying to get everything right, to show the world that old men still had their skills and could do as good a job as those much younger; maybe much better.

It was time to knock off. They closed the doors behind them, having checked everywhere, to make sure all lights were off, and no one had left anything round that might cause a fire. Sid had banned smoking inside, having known one job end in disaster through a half stubbed out fagend.

Paddy Joe vaulted the fence and went through the yard. Deep Hollow was home now. The caravan was dark, so everyone was indoors. The dogs barked as he came by and Mad Cat and Awful rushed to greet him, weaving round his legs. They enjoyed caravan living and shared Paddy Joe's bed, tucking in the back of his knees and mountaineering every time he turned over so that they woke him up.

Sid had excelled himself. The room smelled of savoury food and everyone was enjoying bacon and eggs and cheese potato cakes, the eggs with slightly runny centres, the bacon golden and faintly crisp, the cheese potato cakes a glorious pale toffee brown. With them was a tossed salad of cucumbers and

tomatoes, and when that had gone, there were pancakes filled with jam and cream and flavoured
with lemon juice and grated rind.

"You can come and cook again, Sid," Lisa said.
"It's years since I had a meal cooked by anyone
else."

Tomkin looked at her. He had never thought of
that. Lisa looked tired. Her day was spent in a
constant race against time; time needed for house-
work and cooking and shopping; for puppy feeding
and kennel cleaning and when everyone was at school
the dogs also had to be exercised. Shows, which
had been her great joy, were a thing of the past.
There wasn't time to prepare the dogs, to get them
fit, to exercise them properly. Lisa wouldn't do a job
at all unless she could do it properly; and a dog, for
showing, in her kennels had roadwork as well as a
race in the fields which meant even more time each
day.

"We'll have a rota," Tomkin said. "That will
give you a break. And do the young ones good to
take their turn, instead of being waited on and
food ready for them every night."

Chris made a face at Debbie. Debbie was in a day-
dream and hadn't heard a word, quite unaware that
in two days' time it would be her turn to cook the
evening meal. She was going dancing on Saturday
and her new dress was almost finished. It only
needed trimming, and a bit of embroidery at the
throat. She had worked on it for weeks, studying all
the latest fashions. If her mother would lend her her
gold pendant it would be quite perfect.

Paddy Joe, watching her, knew her thoughts were elsewhere. He was beginning to wonder about people; Sid, who was changing under his eyes from a rather slow, gentle old man into someone who must have been hidden for years; Tomkin, perhaps longing to go back to army days, where everything worked like clockwork, life lived by a time-table, work down on job rotas; and the Colonel. Where was he, looking thoughtfully down at his plate, his eyes remote?

"Haven't had those since my cavalry days," he said unexpectedly. "You'd have enjoyed the horses, Paddy Joe. Thing that sticks in my mind is the end of the day; the last parade before taking them to feed, groom and water them and bed them down for the night. We all lined up, each man standing by his horse. And then the order came. Make much of your horses. And every man patted his horse on the neck three times. A soft thunderclap that sounded over the parade ground and those horses preened themselves, knowing we were proud of them. After that they almost danced to the stables. The mounted police get the same effect though I don't know if they still use the old order. Show an animal that it is needed, that it's making you proud and you have an ally for life."

It had been a long time since the Colonel had so much to say. Sid was doing him good. They were almost of an age.

Sid was never in a hurry to go home. Poll no longer bothered to make him an evening meal. He was never there and she was glad to sit down and rest her feet, on them all day, polishing, cleaning, shopping, never a moment free. She could pick up her knitting and sit and watch her favourite programmes without worrying about Sid's fidgeting, first to go outside and smoke, then to go down the road and look at his silly sheep, though the wool did bring in a bit extra and fair play, he gave it to her. No complaints about that. Sid could repeat his wife's thoughts as if they were his own, but he often wondered if she even guessed his thoughts.

He came out to help Paddy Joe bed the horses. The nights were cooling and all the animals had to be brought in. The foals had been sold, and the mares were in foal again. Prices were improving and people seemed to yearn for horses. Only Thomas played up, pretending to be ten times his size and fierce with it, bucking like a little rodeo horse and then collapsing in anxious adoration when Paddy Joe lost his temper and scolded fiercely: "Stupid pony. Behave!"

Sid laughed as they came into the yard. Thomas kicked at the stable door.

"Enough spunk for ten big 'uns, that little feller," he said. "My sister, Eva, she has a tiny cottage in Wales and breeds those ponies and Welsh ponies. My Bett's gone to live with her, wanting to be with horses too. Poll can't understand Bett, but she got her love of animals from me."

He patted Shadowfax on the muzzle and removed Thomas's teeth from his jacket front. "More buttons to his name than I have hairs on my head," Sid said.

Paddy Joe went into the farmhouse and found Lisa

133

sitting by the fire, a kitten on her knee. The pup she was keeping from Magina's litter was lying on the hearthrug, exhausted by its games with the kit. Wood crackled cheerfully in the grate and the corners were darkened with shadows. Lisa had only a small reading lamp on, throwing a pool of light across her shoulder.

"Put the light on, Paddy Joe. I'm misery membering and it's bad for me. Do you want to do your homework here? I'd be glad of company tonight. It's the anniversary of Derek's death. Ten years ago now, but somehow, it doesn't seem like that." She sighed. "Goodness knows what he'd have made of this place. He wasn't very fond of animals. I sometimes wonder if the dead look down on us, either approving or disapproving; your parents; my husband; if they stand at our shoulders, trying to help; if when I die I'll remain in spirit with Chris and Debbie, watching them, wanting to interfere and never being able to. To say take this road, not that; marry this man, argue not that, seeing the future for them and unable to alter it. Paddy Joe, make me a coffee and make one for yourself, please, I'm getting morbid."

The kitten sat up, small and self important, a tortoiseshell with a merry impish face. It dived off her lap and tapped the puppy on the nose, and then, as the pup woke and stared at it, leaped to the table, from there to the bookcase, darted to the mantelpiece where it flung out a playful paw and toppled one of the little shields won by a long ago dog. Paddy Joe caught the shield, removed the kitten, turned to look at the puppy and hastily rushed it to the door.

"You're learning," Lisa said, laughing. "Only one drop this time; she's improving too. Make sure she does go, Paddy Joe, or she'll play with a stick and drink gallons from the trough and flood the place tonight."

The pup came merrily, her tail waving, and leaped at Paddy Joe, paws on his hands. She loved the world and loved living and was impatient for the future, wanting food quicker than yesterday, wanting out, wanting people, wanting other dogs, wanting cats, and then, if she caught them, not having the least idea what to do with them next. She followed Paddy Joe indoors and settled on the hearthrug with her bone.

Lisa had made the coffee while he was out. He settled down at the table, trying to work out a complicated chemical formula. The room was quiet except for the hiss of the wood and a final sputter from the fire. The kitten was playing gently with Lisa's finger. The pup, intent on her bone, stopped gnawing and looked up at Lisa, a long considering look.

A moment later she launched herself, landing, like a small bomb, in Lisa's lap. The kitten fled, yelling, and the pup tried to force her bone into Lisa's mouth. Lisa, laughing helplessly, attempted to field her off but she was determined.

Paddy Joe was only too glad to have a break from chemistry. He lifted the pup. Lisa pretended to gnaw the bone and handed it back.

"Funny little object," she said. "I've never known a pup do that before. She was obviously thinking when she did it; she'd been staring at me for ages. Poor mistress. No bone."

"Sounds a bit far fetched," Paddy Joe said. "Do you think she meant it like that?"

Even as he spoke the bone was thrust into his hand and the pup looked up at him hopefully. He laughed and pretended to gnaw it. She took it from him, her mouth gentle, and settled again on the rug.

"That's one for advanced training," Lisa said. "Sid's made me feel I ought to get back to some of my old hobbies. I'll take her on and you take on one of Gale's pups. We'll see who does best. A pound for the first to win with a pup next year."

Next year.

Next year he would be seventeen. Next year he would go away to college if all went well. Next year Cockshoot's would be finished and they would be living there. Next year the Colonel was going into the sheep business with Sid as his shepherd and there was already a young collie from a kennel whose stock had high potential, in the empty stall at the end of the stable block, ready for Sid to train. Sid had always wanted to try his hand at the sheepdog trials. The Colonel had always wanted to farm.

Tomkin had always wanted to be a property owner and now he was in partnership with Sid and the Colonel. Sid had the knowhow, and it was soon very obvious that he should have been a farmer; old lore came back from his early days with his father, who had been dedicated and fascinated, showing his stock until times got hard.

"You just keep on hoping, Paddy Joe," Sid said once. "Dreams can come true even when you're a pensioner; so long as you never lose sight of your aims."

But Paddy Joe didn't want to wait over forty years before realising his ambitions; he knew he had to set his goals and make them happen; he had to work. He sighed and went back to his chemistry problem. Time was growing wings, and he would be left behind if he didn't watch out.

Chapter Ten

The nights were dark too early; the weather was increasingly wild. Gale after gale blew up and the winter was a constant din of wind. Some of the horses hated wind and were edgy. Wind made the pups wild, daft little creatures that were hard to handle, too excited to be sensible. Storm and Gale helped to civilise them, along with their own mothers and fathers, but they kept the humans in a constant whirl of activity, escaping from their pens, knocking over the bins and foraging for unspeakable offal, while Magina's pup, now named Cheetah, proved to have an urgent need to eat paper; all kinds of paper: bills, receipts, photographs, the copy of an advertisement Tomkin had been writing for the local paper, the invoice for the fruit trees the Colonel had ordered for the orchard at Cockshoot's. They would be self-sufficient; grow their own produce; keep a goat or two for milk; grow their own animal feed; the plans grew more grandiose daily.

Tomkin wrote them down and Cheetah ate them.

"Hope that's not a sign of our future," he said one morning, having forgotten the pup was in the house. The living room floor was covered with the chewed up contents of the waste paper basket; a quite unrecognisable piece of chewed wood that had obviously come off a piece of furniture; three pigskin gloves now without thumbs or finger tips; Lisa's purse, ripped off its frame, but luckily with the money still intact, and a rug that suddenly boasted a fringe at one end and a number of pieces of chewed wool at the other. In the middle of the floor Pollykitten was busy chewing on what had once been intended for the Sunday joint.

"Someone's going to suffer an upset tummy," Lisa said, coming in with three buttons in her hand. Her new jacket had not been intended to stand up to Thomas's inquisitive teeth. "Why on earth do we have animals?"

"Because you're as nutty as I am," Jake Martin, the gamekeeper said, coming into the room without warning. No one ever knocked at Deep Hollow. They just walked in. No one who didn't belong tried it; the dogs knew friend from stranger and behaved accordingly. Jake was greeted with barks and exploratory sniffs, and then welcomed. He was well known to all the dogs.

"I rescued a raven yesterday," he said. "Daft thing flew into the window glass and stunned itself. I think it thought it was fighting another bird."

"I hope you're not offering it to us," Lisa said. "We seem to grow daily and will soon be bursting at the

139

seams. It's a good job we have the extra fields for the mares at Cockshoot's. This place isn't nearly big enough."

"I'm not offering you the raven. He'll be fit to fly by tonight. He's a bit shaky but he's feeding. It's something else."

"Such as what?"

"There's a stray Alsatian bitch on my patch. She's living in an old foxhole. And she's in milk; came into milk five days ago. I didn't think anything of it at first as she was going somewhere busily and I thought she was on her way home. But then I heard the pups in the foxholes. There are seven of them. Still blind."

"Oh, Jake. What's she feeding them on? Not sheep?"

"No. Mice and rabbit seems to be her diet. I don't know if she's hunting for herself or turned cunning and stealing from a vixen; though that's unlikely; she might just take the leavings."

"They'd be fouled," Tomkin said.

"She's thin as maybe, and wouldn't be that fussy, I'd guess," Jake said. "Lisa, if we can catch her will you take her in? She is purebred, and my guess is she got out and mated with some scruff and they turned her out."

"I could kill people," Lisa said. It wasn't the first time by a long chalk, but they'd always caught the bitch before she whelped. The weather was atrocious; living rough, the pups were sure to die of cold. They couldn't survive. And how to catch her? If she'd been abandoned she wouldn't trust man; and she'd guard her puppies with her life. She'd be as wild as any vixen with cubs to protect.

It was an exercise that needed planning, otherwise the bitch would be scared. If she abandoned the puppies they would die; or she might kill them herself if she were very disturbed by people hunting her. And she would know she was being hunted.

Jake took out his map. On it, meticulously labelled, were the nesting sites of the birds in his care; the haunts of badgers and foxes; the neatly marked in locations of wild birds' nests.

"She's here; the foxhole was abandoned a couple of years ago, when the Hunt was too interested in the place. They found the cubs and the terriers killed them. It hasn't been used since."

"Have you fed her at all?" Lisa asked.

"I've accidentally on purpose put down my sandwich pack where she can get at it," Jake said. "Well filled with meat and chicken and dog biscuits. She tears off the paper in an almighty hurry; she's ravenous. I poured myself a bowl of milk yesterday and then 'forgot' it; she put that down too. I left her an egg beaten up in it this morning, and half a rabbit I shot yesterday. I suspect she's dustbin raiding too, as she has several bits of chicken carcass there, and the chicken has been cooked. She doesn't leave much, though. I found her feeding and she was scared away. I had a good look to make sure she's not taking my game birds."

"Did you handle the pups?" Lisa asked.

"You're joking! And leave my smell on them? Of course not."

Whelping bitches needed a lot of food; good food; extra food. Lisa mixed up a bowlful of meat and biscuit, well laced with vitamin tablets. "Put those in daily and she might not notice if a tranquillising pill was put in as well. Give them for a week to reassure her, to make her feel it is safe to feed. She might not touch this."

Paddy Joe, finding them about to set out in Jake's Land Rover, begged to go too. He was the first to spot the bitch, running through the trees, leaving her den.

"Good," Jake said. "If I take the bowl and put it with my sandwich pack she may accept it at once. She knows my smell now."

Lisa and Paddy Joe watched as he walked into the brambles. He thrust bowl and pack down, and then returned.

"There are still pups there. I can hear them squealing."

"She looked as if she has plenty of milk," Lisa said. "Can we see what happens without her getting wind of us?"

Jake licked his finger and held it up in the air to get the wind direction. No use letting the wind blow their smell to the bitch or she might never return.

"Too fitful," he said. "I think we'd best be on the safe side. I doubt if any other animal is near; she wouldn't tolerate it. And she won't be far away."

He put the car in gear. The bitch had been waiting, knowing the sound of his engine, knowing that he brought food. She was not aware that it was for her. She was stealing, taking what she needed from whatever was near. This time there was dog food in the bowl. She sniffed it suspiciously, but Jake had run his fingers through the mixture and it carried his scent. She knew his scent meant food; and food was safe to eat. She ate greedily, her first good meal for several weeks. She had been living rough for over a month.

Her presence worried Paddy Joe. She had to come from somewhere. Where, was more difficult. He had less time to spend at Cockshoot's now. Exams loomed over him, with the summer coming fast, to decide his fate. He had to do well to gain a place at Glasgow, where he had set his heart on entering the veterinary college. He had visited it one summer, when up in Scotland with the Colonel and Tomkin on a fishing trip. It was set in a park, and the man he had spoken to had taken care to interest him, rousing a passion that had never died.

He went down on the Saturday to look at Cockshoot's, and admire the work now nearing completion. Chris was waiting for him, having been exploring the cellars, which opened out on to a stairway leading down from the basement.

"Have you ever been down?" Chris asked.

Paddy Joe shook his head.

"I've found one answer anyway." Chris pushed open a rickety door. No one had been working here. Sid had explored the cellars from the house, and found them sound, if a bit damp, and had gone no further. The door did not lead through into the main cellar. It had obviously once been a coal room, and there was a chute from the basement into the main cellar through which coal could be shovelled and taken upstairs. It looked highly inconvenient, leading up into the garden by way of rickety, rotting wooden steps. Who'd lug coal up those? Paddy Joe did not realise that some of the cellars were bricked off.

There was straw on the floor, damp and smelling of mould, and an assortment of old bones; a dog bowl, and a ring on the wall, attached to which was a rope. The rope was gnawed through.

"I reckon that bitch was tied up here," Chris said.

There had been a dog there; for days by the look of the place, which no one had cleaned out. There was a rusty bowl full of slimed water, and another bowl, which had never known water at all, in which was some musty food.

"No wonder she escaped," Paddy Joe said. "But who?"

"Moffat was skulking here, wasn't he?" Chris said. "Suppose he's been stealing dogs? Maybe he's mixed up with a gang of criminals. This place could be a super hideout. Let's go scouting round the rest of the cellars and outhouses. We might find some stolen goods."

If there had ever been anything hidden, it had gone long since. Sheds, the barn and the broken down stable yielded nothing. But the cow byre held a surprise; there, stacked as if forgotten by the auctioneers, were a number of odd items. Several stone sinks; another statue of a Roman soldier; an armless and headless Venus, a bird bath, the bowl held up by a naked cherub with revoltingly fat legs and arms, and a sundial, the metal tarnished and words cut deep into the stone: *Procrastination is the thief of time*.

Paddy Joe grinned. Proverbs everywhere.

What a load of useless rubbish.

"Remember how much that other statue fetched?" Chris asked.

Paddy Joe thought back to the day of the auction. The Roman soldier, with sword and helmet; surely it had been the pair to this; looking the other way, if he remembered right.

"Four hundred and twenty pounds," Paddy Joe said, not believing that this could possibly be the same.

"Let's find Tomkin."

Tomkin was engaged on a particularly tricky piece of plastering when they interrupted him, and had no time to listen to the gossip of boys.

"Don't talk rot," he said. "They'd not leave anything behind that was worth selling."

"They left this behind. Maybe they never looked in the cow byre. Who would anyway? Someone cleared the land ages ago and stacked it all there and we get everything that went with the house, don't we?"

"Maybe Moffat cached it there; pinched it from the main sale things, and hoped to come back and get it," Chris said.

"And maybe he didn't." Tomkin put down his trowel. "Show me."

He was pretty sure this was the pair to the other soldier; and the sinks were quite valuable too. Eight of them, worth about twenty pound apiece, Tomkin thought.

He promised to ring the auctioneer and then thought better of it and took the Land Rover and disappeared into town. There could be several hundred pounds worth of stuff there, and maybe those who bought at the sale could be interested now. Might not get as good a price.

The Colonel insisted that everything was brought to Lisa's and put safely under lock and key. News travelled, goodness knew how. Find a small fortune in your byre on Monday and by Tuesday everyone knew you had found a large one and were only waiting for the money to roll in.

Tomkin returned with the auctioneer and they vanished to inspect the find. The sinks were more valuable than they had thought; very old, patterned and attractive, commanding a fortune if sold to Americans who were buying antiques as a new form of status symbol. If it was old, it was worth having.

"When I think of the junk I've chucked out in my life," Tomkin said. "If I'd known, I'd be rolling. An old marble washstand; granma's whatnot; and a pair of the ugliest vases I ever saw. Saw two exactly the same in a shop a few months back going for £250 each. Mad."

Paddy Joe wasn't sure who was mad. The seller of the vases or Tomkin. He was savouring the thought of having been the source of more money to add to their funds. He had been too busy with school work to earn much and with Tomkin for ever working out how much things cost it was impossible not to worry too.

Suppose they ran out and Cockshoot's was not finished.

Suppose he had to go to work when he left school; he had to work with animals. The thought that he might never manage to achieve his ambition was always there, at the back of his mind. Things happened; you couldn't stop them happening. You were caught up in life and sometimes a victim of it, without being able to lift a finger to alter things.

Then his mood would change and he would be sure that life was wonderful, that work was easy, that one day he would be with Tony, first as assistant, then as partner, living in a place he knew well among people he belonged with, doing the work that meant so much to him, perhaps with a falcon to train, and with dogs and cats of his own, and horses. Always horses.

Lisa was taking food out daily, placing it near the fox earth. The puppy noises were louder now; they were obviously strong, and must be healthy. No sickly puppy could make a noise like that. Paddy Joe began to watch too, climbing a tree, so that the bitch could not scent him, or so he hoped. Once she stopped, a paw lifted, sniffing the air. But she ignored the message and went on, and the pups came tumbling out to meet her. They were unsteady, about four weeks old now, Paddy Joe judged and there were seven of them, as rolypoly as any in Lisa's kennels.

There was a footstep, far away, and a twig cracked.

The bitch growled and pushed the pups down into

the ground again, nudging each with her nose. In a few moments there was nothing to show she had ever been there, except for the now empty bowl that she had finished, fast, eating as if the meal was her last, and as if it were also her first. There wasn't a sound from the den.

Jake was walking along the drive.

"I heard you a mile off," Paddy Joe said, as he dropped from the tree.

"I wanted to make sure she heard me," Jake said. "Keep her alert. Someone might find her and shoot her, afraid she'd worry the sheep or boys might harm the pups. They look like pedigree pups to me."

"And me," Paddy Joe said. They were black and fluffy, very like those in Lisa's kennels. Halfbreeds would probably show other colours from birth. They could both be wrong. It wasn't easy to tell.

"Which means, I suspect, she's been stolen, and escaped from the thief," Jake said.

"I'll show you." Paddy Joe led the way back to Cockshoot's, and down into the cellar. Jake looked at the floor, at the rope and the ring in the wall.

"She was kept here, all right," he said.

"Moffat was round here a number of times. We kept seeing him," Paddy Joe said.

"I think Lisa had better put a notice in the dog papers. Someone might claim her. Time we got her and the pups back to safety. I'll be here tomorrow, tell Lisa. If the food is tranquillised we can get the bitch and the pups."

Operation Puppy needed organising.

Tony provided the pills. Lisa made sure the food was extra luscious: the biscuit and dog diet was mixed with gravy from the Sunday roast, with lumps of almost raw steak, the pills hidden inside. Lisa didn't want any slip up. They had to make sure.

"Where are you putting her?" the Colonel asked.

"In the whelping kennel. It's under your nose for one thing; and Major has his pen right beside it and can hear a moth blink; anyone hearing we have her and coming looking will be in for a shock."

The day was hampered by Thomas. The abscess had broken and drained, and twice a Professor from the veterinary hospital had called to see how he was progressing. The dreadful days were over, and Thomas was feeling frisky and putting on flesh again. He wanted attention. He had had so much attention while he was ill, what with. extra feeds and special dainties, to tempt him to eat, and being bathed and fussed over, that to be better and almost ignored was more than he could bear.

Every time anyone went in or out, Thomas called to them.

"That pony's getting above himself," the Colonel said, but all the same went out to stroke the pony and feed him titbits. Shadowfax was jealous and butted. He liked titbits too. He took his share gently, and blew at the Colonel.

It was a grey day, a hint of snow in the air. Winter was here and life for the pups in the earth would be grim. It was a miracle they were alive now. Lisa took the bowl, and climbed into Jake's Land

Rover. Paddy Joe had to go off to school. He wished he could stay behind. He was tempted to pretend he felt sick, but that wouldn't work with Tomkin or Lisa; or the Colonel for that matter. The Colonel, spurred on by Sid, was almost as well as he had been before his stroke. The two old men spent the evening poring over the *Farmer's Weekly*, studying the sheep prices, arguing about the best breed; Sid wanting Welsh Blackfaces, while the Colonel insisted that the only possible breed for them were Southdowns. They spent long hours wondering if the ground was right, if there were trace metals present in the soil, as those were needed for really good sheep rearing; without cobalt in the ground, sheep could die; they pined and drooped and were non-doers always.

The Colonel was so impressed by this information that he spent the days taking soil samples to send away for analysis. If he started a new interest he would make sure he did it right. Sid spent some of his Saturdays collecting books on sheep farming from the library and bringing them back to argue over, until Lisa said that if anyone in the house said "sheep" once more, she would go on strike.

Out on the common the bitch was watching; she now knew that the Land Rover meant food, and she waited for it. Lisa jumped out and put the bowl down beside the den. This time the bitch was on to it almost before Lisa was back inside the vehicle. Jake switched the radio on softly and they waited. The bitch finished her food, and dropped down in front of the den.

"Give her time," Lisa said.

It was an hour before they moved. The bitch was soundly tranquillised. Jake lifted her, putting her on a sack in the back of the Land Rover. She was dirty and she had fleas. She was gaunt, only a memory of what she once had been, but she had still plenty of milk.

The pups were wild.

Jake put in an incautious hand and needle teeth fastened on him. He put on a gauntlet, and the pups were loaded one by one into a large fishing basket, the lid fastened firmly, the whole exercise accompanied by a loud squealing.

"They'll take some civilising," Jake said.

"That depends on the bitch. She knows my smell now;" Lisa said, "it was on her food. I'll mix her food by hand tonight and make sure it's there when she wakes. And she'll be with her pups; it may be all she asks. She must be exhausted. I'll have to wait before I try to clean her up. She looks as if she might be a very nice bitch indeed."

The kennel was ready when they returned, the floor newly cleaned, the box in the corner lined with vetbed blanket to receive its new occupants. Jake put the pups in the box, and the bitch on the ground beside them. They huddled into the corner, away from the man, and from the light that shone through the window. They had spent most of their time in the dark. Lisa found another sack and fixed it to the frame, blacking out the kennel. She put water down by the door and left them.

There wasn't a sound all day.

"Could they die of fright?" Paddy Joe asked when he came home. He had listened, but heard nothing.

"I doubt it." Tomkin was brisk. He had been to find out whether there was a market for Paddy Joe's statue and sinks, and discovered that the buyer of the first statue would buy the second, for the price he had paid at the auction; he reckoned he had a bargain. And the sinks would fetch over thirty pounds each. There was nearly £800 to come.

"I cleared it with the auctioneer," Tomkin said. "No one had looked in the byre and no one knew they were there, so we bought them with the house."

It seemed an odd way to make money. Paddy Joe wondered if he could find any other antiques about the place, and Chris unearthed a number of unlikely items that proved to be totally worthless, and had to be taken to the dump as the binmen saw no reason whatever why they should dispose of bits of old plough, the remains of a rusty pram frame, and a number of motor tyres. Cockshoot's seemed to have been used as a tip by all kinds of people.

"What I need is a metal detector," Chris said, at tea the day the bitch was brought home.

"What you need is to work a bit harder at school," his mother said acidly. "I was talking to your science master yesterday."

Chris glowered at his meat pie.

He was reprieved by a crashing noise. The bitch had woken and was trying to escape.

"Now what do we do?" Lisa asked, as the pups added their frantic squeals to the bitch's persistent hurling against the door.

"Feed her," the Colonel said. "Can you get the food into the run and then release the kennel door without going into the pen?"

"Think so," Tomkin said. He went outside to look and came back to fetch a length of wire, which he fastened round the bolt, making soothing noises that had no effect whatever.

Lisa filled the bowl with everything she could find to tempt the bitch. Meat, biscuit, thick gravy from the marrow bones, and added a big marrow bone for good measure. Paddy Joe put the food down inside the run, and bolted the run door again. The kennel was strong and the wire around it was extra strong as some bitches disliked strangers near their pups and were liable to hurl themselves against the wire mesh, barking their fury. Other dogs were likely to bring out the same response, and all the dogs had to pass to get to the exercise field. It was often bedlam when there was a bitch with puppies in the kennel and run.

Paddy Joe pulled the wire, and the bolt slid open.

The bitch raced out, her eyes wild. She had fallen asleep free, in the long grass and bramble by the den that had been her home for weeks and now was mysteriously brought here to a place that reminded her of the cellar where she had been tied.

Only now she wasn't tied.

She was suddenly free to run into the fresh air; to sniff other dogs, her nose working overtime. The pups came behind her, following her, anxious not to be left. And there was food; she had not been fed well in her previous captivity. This food reminded her of her own home. She sniffed it and began to eat. The pups explored, watchful, ready to run if anything moved. They were not yet very steady on their legs but they were bold, bright eyed and inquisitive. They sat at last in a row in the kennel door, looking out into the yard, where the house lights spilled across the cobbles, patterning it. They had never seen artificial light before.

"How do we get her back into the kennel?" Chris asked.

"We don't. She's been living rough. She'll go for shelter if she wants it. She'll be happier if she's free to come in and out. She won't like being cooped up, but with luck that meal will make her feel sleepy and relaxed and once she realises we are going to keep her and the puppies fed and mean no harm, she should accept us. We'll have to see, anyway."

It was easier than Lisa expected, just so long as she or Debbie brought the food. The bitch was not afraid of women. If Tomkin or the Colonel or Jake or Paddy Joe came near, she launched herself at the kennel run wire, as fierce as any wild animal defending her young.

"Some man has harmed her," Jake said. Paddy Joe was pretty sure he knew who.

There were seven pups. They all looked strong, and were soon running round the pen, playing roughly with one another, rolling and tumbling, as healthy as any carefully reared puppies, except for the fleas, which Lisa dared not treat until the bitch accepted her. The kennel and run would need fumigating.

Tony came to look at them from a distance, and offer advice.

The days passed, and then came a letter from a Hampshire village, in reply to the notice Lisa had put in the dog papers. The writer had had a bitch in whelp stolen from her kennels, about ten weeks before. The times fitted; five weeks running wild and the pups were about five weeks old. Lisa telephoned, and the woman promised to come up at the weekend, as soon as she could organise someone to take over and look after her stock. She was sure the bitch was her best brood bitch, Utschi, and that if only she could come to her, everything would sort itself out. Utschi couldn't be afraid of her owner. She had been house kept. She would never go with strangers, so she must have been doped and then carried off. She was worth several hundred pounds and there was a hundred pound reward for finding her.

Lisa called the bitch in the morning.

"Utschi. Good girl then, Utschi."

The sound of her own name stopped the bitch in mid-stride. She came to the wire, whimpering, her tail wagging very slowly from side to side, uncertain.

"Good Utschi."

Lisa scratched the bitch's head. She had put on flesh and was beginning to show her shape. The pups were eating puppy food, and taking less from her, and the rest from hunting had helped the bitch recover fast. She must have been in fantastic condition to live so rough and do so well for the pups.

"Everything should be fine when her owner

comes," Lisa said. "I wish I could clean her up though."

But when she tried to enter the run, the bitch growled at her. She had not yet learned that it was safe to trust people, even after a fortnight at Deep Hollow, and gentle voices soothing her constantly. Her experiences had unnerved her. She knew that men could be cruel and she could not shake off her fear.

Chapter Eleven

The next day was a Saturday. It was to become memorable in every way, but it started off badly. Thomas was feeling his oats and butted Debbie as she went into the stable to give him his morning feed. Her feet slid from under her on wet ground, and she fell heavily, knocking over the ready filled dog bowls waiting to be given out to the occupants of the kennel block next to Thomas. Loose dogs converged on the food at once, and Debbie shouted, knowing that there would be trouble if they ate all the feed intended for fifteen dogs. Storm, Gale, and Magina were the only ones free.

Paddy Joe and Tomkin ran, grabbing at collars, hauling off dogs determined to savour this unexpected feast. The Colonel went to fetch a broom and Lisa, faced with all the feeds to prepare again, shouted at every one in turn, knowing she would now be short of time all day, racing through the hours, trying frantically to make up for lost time.

Debbie was more concerned with her ruined tights, her dirtied dress and the fact that Paul was due to fetch her and she had now to change all her clothes and her only other decent outfit was at the cleaners. Chris helped no one by laughing at Debbie, and announcing he had promised to help Sid with some plastering at Cockshoot's.

"No one in this place does a hand's turn," Lisa stormed, and then discovered she had only two of the cats as audience. The other cats were busy licking the cobbles, while the Colonel tried to thrust them away with the broom.

Nobody noticed that the stable door was ajar, except Thomas, who, annoyed by all the noise, trotted out when everyone was busy elsewhere, and finding the gate left open by Debbie, who had arranged to meet Paul at the end of the lane, and had raced off afraid he would not wait, trotted out to explore the world.

The world was interesting, and Thomas trotted on.

It was Paddy Joe who found the empty stable, and grabbed his bicycle and pedalled off fast, praying no one else noticed that Thomas had gone. Luckily it had been raining and Thomas preferred grass verge to road. His small hoofprints were plain to see.

He had found another open gate. Paddy Joe looked at the pony, head half way through an open window, apparently fascinated by what was going on inside. There was no one in the kitchen but a large batch of cakes had been put on the sill to cool. It looked as if the cottage owner had been baking for a multitude. She had in fact been making the food for a Women's Institute party. It was obvious that Thomas had made major inroads into the cakes. Paddy Joe waited, but no one came. He wrote a hasty note saying, "Terribly sorry, it was our horse," and left it beside the cakes, having to return to add "Deep Hollow" so that the occupant knew who to blame. There were other ponies in the village though none were quite so mischievous as Thomas now he was fit.

Paddy Joe led the pony back. Thomas trotted meekly beside the bicycle, good as any pony could be, never put a hoof wrong, an angelic expression on his face.

"Isn't he sweet?" a girl said, as they passed.

Paddy Joe grinned.

It wasn't the word he had in mind for Thomas at that moment. He was relieved to see that everyone was busy and Thomas hadn't been missed, though he expected the phone to ring any moment and an irate cake baker to demand reparation. The cottage owner kept goats. Paddy Joe's note had blown away and was never even seen by her, and her two goats were blamed. She should have closed the kitchen window. It wasn't as if she didn't know the hazards of animals around her.

By the time Utschi's owner arrived the day had degenerated into a wild scramble to get through. Lisa had put bread and meat on the table and made coffee, and everyone was having a help-yourself stand-up lunch. Paddy Joe had cut himself several doorsteps. Lisa had been into Debbie's room, looking for her belt, and found the bed unmade, and clothes everywhere, and that the belt must be on Debbie, as was Lisa's best coat. She was vowing vengeance when Jenny Lester walked into the kitchen.

"I'm sorry. I couldn't make anyone hear," she said. "I'm Utschi's owner."

"It's bedlam," Lisa said. "Would you like to eat before you go and see if it is Utschi? If it isn't you'll be too unhappy to eat; and if it is, you will probably be too busy!"

"I've waited ten weeks," Jenny said. "Another twenty minutes won't make much odds; I'm a bit tired from driving, and I'm also afraid to go and look. It might not be Utschi."

Lisa made sandwiches, and poured coffee. Jenny was much younger than they expected, a tall woman with beautifully cut dark hair lying sleekly against her head, dark brown eyes that now were anxious, and a mouth that was obviously used to laughing. The dogs piled on to her, and in no time at all she had kittens on her knee and another on her shoulder.

"It's just like home," she said. "We live in a madhouse too. I'm getting married soon and my own ambition is to have it all just the same. I can't bear being without animals. It was awful when Utschi vanished."

"During the night?" Lisa asked.

"No. We were all out. The dogs were in a padlocked run, and no one had ever interfered with them before. The wire had been cut. We found three doped dogs and Utschi gone. Someone must have known she was in whelp."

160

"What would they do with the pups? They couldn't be sold as pedigrees without her papers," Paddy Joe said.

"They could. There's quite a racket going on. Dealers buy in puppies from breeders who have quite good stock; no one but the breeder and the dealer knows how many pups were in the litter. So if there were only four, eight puppies are registered, four of them having the wrong parents, but much better parents than their own, or, in the case of Utschi's puppies, perhaps not so good as their own; but they fetch fifty or sixty pounds each and the breeder takes a cut as well from the extra puppies. It's not widely done, but it is done. And I think that is what would have happened to Utschi if you hadn't found her. I know a number of people near us who have had dogs go missing. One bitch died; the vet thinks from an accidental overdose that wasn't intended."

"What a horrible thought," Lisa said. "I never thought of dog thieving for a profit. Just as something perhaps silly and casual; steal a dog and sell it in a pub some distance away for a bit of ready money."

"This looks as if it is organised," Jenny looked out of the window. The whelping kennel was hidden, but a footfall sounded in the yard and the dogs barked.

"That *is* Utschi. I'd know her bark anywhere. Where is she?"

"I'll show you."

Food was forgotten. Lisa and Jenny went out into

the yard, and the others followed, wondering if Jenny were right.

Utschi was lying in the corner of the run watching her puppies play. They were becoming more used to people now, but still hesitated and did not come to the wire to greet everyone as normal puppies did.

Jenny called softly.

"Utschi. Utschi girl. Utschi."

The bitch leaped to her feet, looking for the voice. She saw Jenny, caught her scent and hurled herself at the wire.

Jenny opened the gate and went inside. Utschi leaped at her, licking her face, and then knees bent, tail almost coming off, ears back in adoration, she ran round and round Jenny, squealing in welcome, unable to express all she felt. Jenny knelt and put her arms round the bitch.

"She's full of fleas. We haven't been able to touch her," Lisa said apologetically, but Jenny didn't even hear. They left the two together and went back indoors. A few minutes later Jenny came into the room, Utschi at her side, a completely different animal, transformed, in contact with her mistress, back to her former gentle self.

"We'll have to clean her up before you take her away," Lisa said. "You'll be taking back a host of fleas. She lived very rough."

"We can take her into the stable and bath her there, and then bring her into the warm and dry her," Paddy Joe said.

"Would you like to stay overnight?" Lisa asked.

162

"We might be able to clean the pups too with you here to reassure Utschi. We'd love to have you. And we can get to know Utschi as she really is."

Utschi didn't mind what Jenny did to her. Bathed and towelled until she was almost dry she came happily into the kitchen to lie by the fire, while Storm and Gale watched jealously from the other side of the room.

"Those are very well bred pups," Jenny said. "Would you like to keep one? I bred her on working lines, back to one of the first dogs to be a champion both in Beauty and Obedience; Champion Terrie of Glenvoca. I've always been interested in the way heredity shows up in puppies and wondered how far a dog's influence will stretch through the generations. Terrie is way back in Utschi's ancestry as well as in the dog who was father to the pups; so the pups with luck might make very good workers as well as looking good. I'll let you have your pick. I can't tell you how grateful I am. And of course there's the reward money too."

"We don't want that," Lisa said.

"You're getting it," Jenny was determined.

She helped Lisa with the kennel jobs, and the day recovered its tranquillity, so that by supper time everyone was relaxed and at ease. Utschi had gone back to her pups, but cried to return to Jenny. The pups were warm and fed and content and more than halfway weaned, so that Utschi was to spend the night by Jenny's bed, rather than be parted again. The bitch did not take her eyes off her mistress for one moment and every time Jenny moved,

Utschi was by her side, watching her.

"It will be a long time before she feels safe again," Tomkin said.

He had cooked the supper; a meal fit for a king, he said, having made an enormous casserole of meat and onions, parsnips, leeks and carrots, flavoured deliciously, served on a huge bed of boiled rice, with green beans grown in the summer and deep frozen. It was followed by frozen raspberries and thick Cornish cream, and tiny pancakes spread with jam and sprinkled with lemon. Debbie was still out, but Sid had joined them, and so had Dan Martin, Jake's son, who was telling an absurd story about Rack and Ruin, his father's pointers, who had found their first hedgehog and spent the day trying to summon up enough courage to go near it.

"Cockshoot's will soon be ready for us to move in," Tomkin said. "Another four weeks, and we can start decorating the rooms we want to use first. And then we go places."

"It sounds as if it will be a wonderful place one day," Jenny said. "I haven't nearly enough ground. I'd love to breed horses as well as dogs. It will be even more difficult when I marry as we have to start off in a small way; maybe, one day...."

Paddy Joe was listening, saying little himself. He seemed to be shown different things almost every day; starting again, on your own, with no one to back you and no money behind you ... but a way of your own to make, perhaps new ground to break, perhaps to improve on what your parents and grandparents did. No one could do it for you. Tomkin's words echoed in his mind. "You'll be on your own, Paddy Joe. We've done all we can. Now it's up to you. I can't learn for you; I can only tell you that fire's hot and knives cut and if you play with either you get hurt."

"Show me your falcon, Paddy Joe," Jenny said.

Paddy Joe had missed the conversation, but he guessed that somehow Khan had been mentioned, and opened the door to lead Jenny outside. Utschi, following close, growled softly and Storm, coming to the door, began to bark. Gale's higher pitched barking was followed by pandemonium from the kennels. The wind was high and at first Paddy Joe thought they had gone wind crazy, barking at nothing or perhaps sounds that only they could hear.

And then he realised they were barking at sounds that he hadn't heard before, as from the direction of Cockshoot's came a wild yell and the sound of breaking glass.

"Trouble at Cockshoot's," he shouted, and Tomkin came running.

"Fetch a torch," he called to Lisa.

Debbie came into the farmyard, racing as if the wild hunt were on her heels.

"We came past Cockshoot's," she said. "They are breaking the windows there. Paul's gone for the police. He thought it would be quicker to phone from the call box than come on here. He dropped me at the gate. There are several men there; be careful."

"We'll be careful," Tomkin said grimly. He was opening kennel doors.

"Find them, dogs!"

Storm led the way, pelting into the darkness.

"Suppose they bite," Paddy Joe said.

"They won't and frankly I wouldn't care if they did. I don't know how many men there are but six large dogs might make them think again."

Paddy Joe vaulted the fence, Chris and Tomkin behind him, Tomkin coming more slowly. The Colonel had gone for his shotgun. He walked painfully through the gate. The dogs were baying, working as a pack, and there were shouts and curses from the men, carried on the wind.

Someone raced across the field, Gale behind him. She flew at his shoulders and brought him down, so he lay on his face, breathless, while the bitch circled him, snarling, nothing like her normal gentle self.

"Keep him there, Gale," Paddy Joe said.

There was the sound of a siren in the distance, followed by another, and a few minutes later there were policemen everywhere with torches that lit the scene.

They were at the rear of the house which had very big windows, and all of these were smashed. Glass was everywhere, but the dogs had not gone near. One man was perched on top of the oil tank, with Storm barking furiously below him. Magina had penned another against an angle of the wall. He too was afraid to move, while Magina circled him, out of range of his arms, instinctively knowing exactly how to menace him without going too close or coming into range.

Utschi was nowhere to be seen.

Jenny was calling her, her voice anxious.

Then came a yell of utter terror.

Paddy Joe and one of the policemen raced round the corner of the house. Moffat lay flat on the ground, with Utschi raging around him. Every time he moved she snarled more loudly. He knew enough to lie quite still, praying at the top of his voice to a God he had long ago forgotten.

"Get her off me," he shouted.

"Utschi, leave." Jenny's voice was firm, loud enough to sound above the bitch's snarling. Utschi came to her mistress but stood with hackles raised, her face a mask of anger, the low pitched growl never ceasing.

"She wants to kill me," Moffat said. His voice was only a memory of his usual cocky self. He was covered in mud, both his hands were grazed from gravel and one of them cut on glass.

"Not sure you don't deserve it," the policeman said. "What's the idea? Think you could get away with this lot without being found out?"

"We would 'ave done with that wind blowing, if the dogs 'adn't 'eard us," Moffat said. He looked uneasily at the Colonel who had the gun held as if he were going to shoot. "It was only a bit of fun," Moffat said.

"Funny idea of fun," the policeman said. By now there were five men under arrest, being escorted to the cars, while the dogs came back and stood together, watching. Storm growled menacingly as Moffat passed him. Utschi did not relax for a moment.

There was little that could be done to remedy the damage till it was light. If only it didn't rain in and spoil the floors and plaster. Two of the policemen stayed behind, one, with his dog, to patrol the house till morning, and ensure there was no further damage, the other to look around.

"Do you know what that was all about?" he asked Paddy Joe. The Colonel and Tomkin had gone to switch lights on and investigate inside and make sure there was no damage other than broken windows. The dog handler and his dog were looking for signs of fire.

"I can show you one thing," Paddy Joe said, and took the man down to the cellar where Utschi had been kept. Jenny followed. Utschi stood in the doorway, trembling, not wanting to go any further, even though Jenny was there.

"That's where this bitch was kept," he said. "She was stolen while she was in whelp. She escaped and we found her and her puppies; she'd been living wild."

"I heard about that from Jake," the policeman said. "Are you sure she was stolen?"

"She's my bitch," Jenny said. "She vanished while we were out one afternoon. The place was broken into. Whoever came in knew just what they wanted; she's a very good bitch indeed. Others have gone from around us, and one dog that was doped too heavily died. If you contact the police in my area you'll hear about more than I know as they said there had been a number of cases, in a fifty-mile area around me. I was just one of a number;

168

and I've been lucky. I've got bitch and puppies back."

"She looks a lovely animal," the policeman said. "We'd better go back to Deep Hollow and try and make sense of this lot. I'll want statements from everyone. I expect we'll find out more from the men they've taken into custody. Heaven knows how they expected to get away with it."

"Moffat stole Utschi," Paddy Joe said. "She knew him. That's why she singled him out; and he knew her. He was terrified of her. And Moffat isn't scared of dogs. He's banned from owning them, because he's cruel to them, but he isn't scared. Any other dog, he'd have kicked. He's tried to kick Storm before now. I don't know why he's never been bitten."

"Maybe he has," Tomkin said.

"We've had our eye on Moffat for long enough," the policeman said. "If we can tie him in with dog stealing ... there are a few other things we'd like to know about."

"I'd like to know why he wanted Cockshoot's and why they are still trying to scare us off," the Colonel said.

It was late and everyone was tired. There were dogs to shut in and dogs to feed; there were stable doors to bolt, and both Shadowfax and Thomas had been upset by all the din and had to be fussed and soothed before either would settle. The mares, in the distant stable, were quiet. But Tomkin checked everything twice, and even then went to bed uneasy, leaving Storm beside an open window in the caravan to give warning of any further trouble.

Paddy Joe lay awake for a long time, listening to the wind, and the noises around him. The sounds were odd; the stamp of the horses, the noise of dogs, the sudden flurry as some of the pups woke and played together, growling and biting one another and making small mock barks, wakened by a brilliant moon that misled them into thinking it was time to get up.

An owl called.

That at least was familiar.

Perhaps Cockshoot's was the meeting place of the gang; perhaps they robbed banks as well as stealing dogs; perhaps they were terrorists, and there was a hoard of guns and ammunition hidden somewhere. Perhaps Moffat was the leader of a huge criminal organisation, though that didn't seem likely. He might be in disguise, pretending to be a down-at-heel farmer going slowly bankrupt, instead of a big tycoon. It could all be a cover for something else.

Diamond smuggling.

Jewel robberies.

Paddy Joe's ideas became more and more extreme as sleep came nearer and when sleep did come he spent half the night chasing unseen men who shouted, while Storm and Gale raced further and further away from him and wouldn't come back, however hard he called.

He was thankful when Tomkin shook him awake, and he found a thin winter sun shining and Sid standing in the doorway, blazing with anger because of their ruined work and all the windows to do again as well as clearing up the debris.

"It could have been worse," Tomkin said. It was small consolation.

Chapter Twelve

"It's a daft story," the Colonel said next evening, after a day spent with the police, looking round Cockshoot's and finding out just why Moffat and his friends were trying to sabotage the place. He had brought one of the policemen back with him.

"They started by using the place as cover for stolen dogs; Utschi is one of a long line of them. When the bitch had whelped they sold her as well as the pups. Lots of them are doing duty in garages all over the country. I've a list now and some of them will be returned to their owners. They could get as much as fifty pounds for the bitch and forty each for the puppies that did go to a dealer and were sold with false pedigrees at eighty pounds a time. Nice profits all round. The place is isolated, and no one would ever hear them; or if they did, would think it was one of your dogs and not bother to investigate. And then you started to be interested in the place, which meant they had nowhere safe to hide the bitches.

If Utschi hadn't escaped they might have risked going on, but trying somewhere else if they couldn't scare you off."

"It seems ridiculous to buy the place just for that," Tomkin said. He had been busy all day; he had helped Jenny bath the pups and then load them all into her estate car, Utschi sitting on the passenger seat, determined never to leave her mistress again. Once she was reunited with Jenny, her fierceness had vanished and she had learned to trust everyone at Deep Hollow during her days with them.

"There's a lot more to it than that. Someone else found out about their activities while he was looking at Cockshoot's. He was blackmailing them. Cockshoot's was just what he wanted for a Country Club, and there's talk of a new motorway at the edge of the land, as well as the golf course. It could be worth a great deal more than you paid for it. Moffat hadn't realised you were interested or ready to go up to the price you put in and hadn't asked how much he could bid; so he dropped out of the bidding and was in dire trouble for that, with orders to scare you off at any price and make you re-sell." The policeman sipped his coffee. "He's a stupid man; he didn't know how to go about it. The story of subsidence and of opencast mining in your old place didn't come from him; they thought if you couldn't sell one you wouldn't have money for the other. Then Utschi vanished and you found her and Moffat was scared that something would lead you back to him. The idea last night was to so wreck your work that you gave up in despair; they were all set to flood the place. There was a hose connected to the bathroom tap, but no one had had time to turn it on."

The Colonel laughed.

"It's not funny," Lisa said indignantly.

"We haven't connected the water yet," the Colonel said. "The only water came from here or the well. They couldn't flood it. There's all the piping to be done from the water main. The men are starting next Tuesday. Though if they had set fire to the place, we would have been in dire trouble. Cockshoot's has never had mains water or main drainage."

"You should find that you can sell part of the land for the golf course without too much of your own land vanishing," the policeman said. "I don't know exactly what kind of money they pay, but it's good money, I'm told. The road won't come too near, but there's to be a flyover, which will encroach on that bit of wood. I've seen the plans, after hearing Moffat's story. He won't bother you again."

Paddy Joe went out into the night.

He could hear Khan rustling on his perch and went in to talk to the bird and stroke him. Tomorrow Khan was to fly free. They had been training him to hunt for himself and he was now expert. It was cruel to keep him tame when the wild sky called to him and he was more and more reluctant to return to the lure. In the morning the jesses would come off, and Paddy Joe's Christmas present to his bird would be freedom. He couldn't bear the thought. Khan was part of his life – Khan was magnificence, a regal beauty, to own for ever.

Freedom.

In less than a year's time he too would be free; free to start a new career, with enough money now, and no worry about the Colonel and Tomkin being unable to manage if he did not help. Sid and his friends and the Colonel and Tomkin had formed a syndicate; they were all to farm together and the sheep were being selected, some Blackfaces and some South-downs; one flock for Sid and another for the Colonel and fierce rivalry between the two.

Life changed so much all the time.

Debbie had come into the shed behind him.

"Will you let him go?" she asked.

Paddy Joe nodded.

"We all need to be free," he said, recognising her need too. He had once had dreams about Debbie, but Debbie had never included him in hers. He closed the door behind him. He needed to be alone. He could not own Khan, could not keep him prisoner when the wide sky called him, any more than he could stay here for ever with Tomkin and the Colonel, when his own life was waiting for him, beyond their horizons.

"Nobody's entirely free," Debbie said. She had been thinking too, and followed Paddy Joe. "You have the Colonel and Tomkin to consider; I have mother; if she were ill, or couldn't manage, I'd not be able to turn my back. Stay here, there are the dogs and horses, demanding attention all the time. Go away, and there's something else; a job to be done, money to be earned to live; if I marry then there's a husband and maybe children to consider;

where's the freedom for any of us, Paddy Joe? Free for what?"

"To make choices," Tomkin said, from the darkness beyond the door, "or to plan and make your plans come true. Sounds silly, but it's the little choices that we make that have most influence. If I hadn't come to help your guardian, Paddy Joe, would he have taken on a boy of twelve and Storm by himself? Would he have been friends with your grandmother? If you hadn't found Black Bitch on the river bank and cared for her you'd never have met anyone at Deep Hollow. You could have gone away and left her. Then our lives would have taken a different road."

"A very different road," the Colonel said. He had come out to the caravan, and stood unobserved, also listening. Storm and Gale were waiting by the caravan door knowing that before they went to bed they would have four biscuits each from the dog tin. Both were salivating expectantly. The Colonel went inside.

Debbie and Paddy Joe leaned companionably on the field gate, looking at the silhouette of Cockshoot's. Debbie was thinking aloud.

"If Tomkin hadn't wanted to own property; if father hadn't died; and your parents and grandmother hadn't died; if we hadn't bought Cockshoot's, then we'd have never known Sid; and the Colonel might have drifted into real old age. Now he's like a kid with a new bicycle, have you noticed, Paddy Joe?"

Paddy Joe had noticed. Sid and the Colonel,

eagerly planning, seemed younger daily, excitement mastering them just as much as it did him.

Tomkin came back from the house. He had been in to arrange the next day's work with Lisa. He had very sharp ears.

"They are like kids," Tomkin said, drifting into the conversation again, as he often did, wanting desperately to help Paddy Joe face an adult world, and not wanting to lecture too much. "You'll find, all your life, Paddy Joe, that inside, you don't change, unless you let life get you down. You'll always feel the same age as you do now; do you feel any older than last year?"

"I understand more, I think," Paddy Joe said.

Tomkin smiled to himself in the darkness. It was an answer that pleased him. Paddy Joe was growing up.

They stood together companionably, saying nothing, each busy with thoughts of the future. Tomkin smug as a cat that had eaten cream, thinking of his stake in Cockshoot's, of the farm they would build in the years to come, an inheritance for Paddy Joe who was all the family he had. He would never admit to his fierce pride in his employer's ward. But his plans were always made with Paddy Joe in mind. He had been given a son by proxy and enjoyed teaching him.

Paddy Joe was half aware of that; but his own thoughts were on the next years, on college and more animals, on the releasing of Khan next day. Debbie was dreaming of a bridal dress and a church wedding, but the man's face was not clear; it was a dream of a future, a dream of a dream without substance.

Storm nosed Paddy Joe's leg.

It was time for bed.

Paddy Joe did not want the morning to come, or to let the falcon go.

But morning dawned clear, and Tomkin, at breakfast, looked up at the sky, and nodded to Paddy Joe.

Khan came to his fist as if he belonged there for ever, and Paddy Joe rubbed the soft feathers of the bird's chest. He went out alone, beyond the wood to the high rise of the downs. There was a shimmer of grey in the sky, masking the blue. It was Christmas Eve.

Tomorrow would be Christmas.

In the building behind him were his own animals; Gale and Storm and the pup from Utschi that Lisa had given to him for his own. He would not have time to train her soon; that would be Tomkin's task and Tomkin was so eager that Paddy Joe knew he had another sacrifice to make. The pup would be his Christmas present to Tomkin. Much as he wanted another to train. He would never have enough dogs about him.

They crested the hill.

Paddy Joe had shut the dogs away, ignoring their mournful howls.

He had grown to love this bird; had spent hours with him, teaching him how to hunt and now he was letting him go to his own future.

He removed the jesses and took off the little bell.

Khan stood proud on his fist and for a moment

the bird and boy looked at one another as if the bird understood that with his symbols of bondage gone, he was free for always.

Paddy Joe raised his fist.

The powerful wings beat as the bird soared into the sky. Up and up until he was only a blur against the wintry sun. Paddy Joe watched him, until there was nothing more to see.

He turned homewards, back to his own unknown future, knowing that this was the first of many sorrows, that he could not easily fill the niche this bird had carved in his life, nor find again the pleasure he had taken in watching it dive back to his lure.

The rook feathers were hung on the shed hook.

He took them down. He would never need them again.

There were paws against his thigh. One of Magina's pups had come to take the feathers from him. She ran off with her trophy, taking it into her pen to hide it in the corner, away from the other pups.

Debbie was rushing out of the yard, due to meet Paul.

Thomas leaned his head against Paddy Joe's shoulder and neatly removed a button.

"Stop brooding, Paddy Joe," Tomkin said. "You should have been ready for that. Give me a hand."

Paddy Joe lifted the bucket and took it into the stable, pouring the feed into the manger. Thomas butted him, and started to feed as if he had never been fed before. Shadowfax rattled an impatient hoof against the partition.

179

Lisa called from the house, wanting help with the puppy kennels.

There was work to do and the future to prepare for and another year would soon begin.

Paddy Joe fetched the yard broom and began to whistle the tune of "Those were the days, my friend ... we thought they'd never end. ..."

Tomkin, looking out of the stable, saw the Colonel and gave him the thumbs up sign. One set of problems had ended. More would come, but today was fine for all of them and tomorrow would be Christmas.

His whistle picked up Paddy Joe's theme, and the Colonel joined them, recalling a skill long forgotten, outdoing both of them.

He changed the tune.

Lisa, bringing out the bowls of puppy food, joined in the chorus:

"We wish you a Merry Christmas and a Happy New Year."

Chris, dismounting from his bicycle, looked at them in amazement and then dived a hand into his pocket and solemnly awarded them a penny each.

Lisa laughed.

"Time for coffee, and we'll toast the future with it," she said.

She looked across at Cockshoot's.

"This time next year, you'll be living there. I wonder what else will have happened by then?"

"Gale will have had her pups; I'll be at college; Debbie will have left school; Chris will be bottom of the class."

Paddy Joe stopped for breath and to dodge a thrown paperback, and Thomas called companionably across the yard.

"And Thomas will have disposed of another hundred or so buttons," Chris said.

Thomas's shrill whinny, on hearing his name, seemed to agree with them.

A shadow flew across the yard.

Storm barked.

Paddy Joe walked outside.

Khan was waiting on the wall. He flew to Paddy Joe's shoulder.

"He's chosen to live with us," Tomkin said.

Paddy Joe took the bird, and put him on his block. Khan might have come for love – he might only have come for food, but he had chosen for himself. From now he would fly high and come home of his own free will. He was not a prisoner. He was part of the family.

Paddy Joe couldn't have had a better Christmas present.